Whores, Love and Pistols in the Wild West

First Edition

Published by The Nazca Plains Corporation
Las Vegas, Nevada
2008

ISBN: 978-1-934625-86-6

Published by

The Nazca Plains Corporation ®
4640 Paradise Rd, Suite 141
Las Vegas NV 89109-8000

PUBLISHER'S NOTE
Whores, Love and Pistols in the Wild West is a work of fiction created wholly by *Tim Desmondes's* imagination. All characters are fictional and any resemblance to any persons living or deceased is purely by accident. No portion of this book reflects any real person or events.

Cover Photos, SteveMC and MIL
Art Director, Blake Stephens

Dedication

They were all heroes, especially those we call the heroines. The women who braved the virile world of the Wild West had to exceed the men bravery to make it.

My great grandmother, Carrie, was a woman who could tote a gun and fight the elements while at the same time raising three sons, all of whom did her proud.

Here's to you, Carrie Lott.

Tim Desmondes

Whores, Love and Pistols in the Wild West

First Edition

Tim Desmondes

Table of Contents

PART TWO
CALAMITY JANE SHAGS WILD BILL HICKOK

Introduction

The Wild West gave us some of the most memorable characters in our history.

The West was where those free spirits from the East migrated to wrestle and tame a precarious wilderness

Calamity Jane, Big Nose Kate, and their men, Wild Bill Hickok and Doc Holliday, were rough, tough, earthy, and bold.

Above all, they were survivors.

If you enjoy reading about kind, gentle, soft-spoken ladies and gentlemen, this isn't the book for you.

If you like stories about loud, rowdy, raucous, quick-on-the-draw, lusty heroes, heroines, lawmen and outlaws, both male and female, read on.

These are the people of the Wild West, an era that will always be legendary to Americans.

Tim Desmondes

PART ONE

BIG NOSE KATE

DOES DOC HOLLIDAY

Chapter One

MOSTLY ABOUT ME

Doc Holliday? You want to know about that good-for-nothing, lying, cheating, cold-blooded lunger card shark? That son of a bitching bastard who'd as soon shoot you as look at you?

Yeah, I knew him. And I loved him.

And God help me, I'll love that bastard until the day I die.

Me? I'm Big Nose Kate Elder. And I'm a whore.

Let's get that straightened out before I tell you about Doc.

Now, that epithet I carry. Yeah, the "Big Nose" part.

I wear this aristocratic nose with pride. My ancestors were Norman-French aristocracy – way back. And I am as proud as they were of the ducal nose.

There are a lot of Kates out here in the West. But, I am the only one with the aristocratic nose.

And my last name, Elder. The Elders were among the first colonists to settle Rhode Island. They were a very pious bunch. We made our fortune in the slave and rum trade. My family back East is rich as Hell.

I guess that takes care of the name I go by. Big Nose Kate Elder.

But, you might ask, what am I?

I already told you.

I am a whore. I practice the most ancient profession of all. And, I might add, the most necessary one.

What I want you to know, though, is that I am not a two-bit whore.

There's a passel of two-bit whores out here. They're a necessary commodity with all the healthy young miners, cowboys, buffalo hunters, gamblers and soldiers who populate the West.

I respect the two-bit whores.

But I'm not one of them.

Those sisters practice their trade in whorehouses and work for madams, pimps, or mackerels.

That's not for me. I am an independent operator. And for a standard treatment of what I sell it will cost you four-bits – up.

I'll tell you how I became a whore.

.....

It really started when my parents found out I was a "problem child."

My very earliest memory, way before I was old enough to start school, is a very happy recollection. I was sucking the cock of my little brother.

I just always knew I loved cocks and balls.

I liked them. I liked the feel in my mouth. I liked the smell of that little thing. I liked the taste. I liked how happy it made Willy.

I don't have any idea how many days, weeks, or months passed by while I played and sucked on Willy's wee-wee. But one day, Mother walked in on us when I had a mouthful of both his cock and his empty little ball-sack.

And, immediately, I was a *problem child.*

.....

I never got over my taste for cocks and balls.

(And subsequently learned to love fellers who love tits, cunt, and ass. I may mention that later on.)

As I grew older, I became adept at the game of "I'll show you mine if you'll show me yours." I played it with girl and boy playmates.

I got more of a charge out of it with the boys. But it was also quite entertaining with my girl playmates as well.

What I was really good at was making sure no adults ever caught us.

You'd be surprised how popular I was among the girls and boys in our neighborhood (and beyond).

(Some of you, I see, would not be surprised at all.)

My parents got enough feedback from some of their nosey friends to realize they could find themselves with a large potential problem when I hit puberty. Something would definitely have to be done about my reproductive equipment.

Since they were rich, they could afford the best.

There was a specialist in Utica, in upper New York State, who ran a regular practice of "fixing" problem children, both girls and boys.

So my parents took me to the clinic in Utica and got me spayed well before I would have had my first period.

I was wise enough to appreciate what was going on.

I was even more grateful after I entered my profession.

One thing a whore definitely does not need is to get knocked up. And the only positive way to be sure is to get some doctor to convert the nursery into a playroom.

Thank you, Mommy and Daddy.

. . . . .

When I was sweet sixteen, my folks sent me off to New Hampshire. There's a finishing school up there that will accept problem children. It's still there. It's called Miss Claybourne's Academy for Young Ladies. You could look it up if you have a daughter whose interests parallel mine.

I got a good education at Claybourne's.

Music, literature, sewing, manners…

Oh, yes. And also the fine art of cunt eating.

We girls had ourselves a time at night in the dormitory, let me tell you.

I got to really enjoy sucking tittie and eating pussy. Licking a stiff clit is one Hell of a time.

Naturally, my preference for cocks and balls remained paramount. But there were neither cocks nor balls at Miss Claybourne's. And it was not tough settling for tits and cunt.

.....

When I graduated from Miss Claybourne's, I had no intention of returning to the strictures of life in Providence. And I could hear the sigh of relief from my parents when I told them I was not planning to move back in with them.

They told me they loved me, and would provide me a hefty allowance for as long as I lived. A trust fund was set up for me at the Ainsley Trust Company of Providence.

They did not suggest that I keep in touch with them. I just had to let the Trust know where I was and it would send me my monthly stipend.

I was now an adult. I was horny, spayed, educated, and looking to enter my chosen profession.

So I left New England on a train headed for Texas. And I was thrilled and excited as I thought of all the cock there was out there in that male population that dominated the Wild West.

.....

When I was at the academy, we girls did more than just suck each other's titties and munch each other's pussy. We shared information about the opportunities that awaited us after graduation.

So when that train pulled into the Dallas station with me in it, I knew the score.

In the West, a girl could always get herself a job at a whorehouse. As you know, that wasn't for me.

There are saloons and dancehalls in every settlement as well. Some of the saloons have dancehalls as part of the entertainment. Some don't.

But what they all have are cribs and/or fuckrooms upstairs.

A dolly can arrange with the management for use of a crib or a fuckroom.

A crib is a room with a bed and a basin that can be used by any girl registered with the house to entertain a client. The house takes care of stocking the room with towels, wash cloths, and sheets.

You take your man upstairs, take the agreed upon sum of money from him, service him, and split the take with the saloonkeeper, twenty-five percent to him, seventy-five percent to yourself.

There's a temptation to hold out on the management. But men are such loudmouths that word gets back to the manager and your ass gets kicked out of the place and word gets around to the other 'keepers.

Not worth it.

The other way to go, instead of using a crib, is to rent a fuckroom.

A fuckroom looks just like a crib. It's upstairs and is furnished with a bed and a basin. The dove furnishes her own towels, wash cloths, and sheets.

She pays anywhere from five to fifty dollars a day to the 'keeper. That room is hers. No sharing with the other girls.

So that's the difference between a crib and a fuckroom.

That information is in case you ever decide you want to go into the business. Or, as we call it, the profession.

I'd done my research before I ever got to Dallas. I knew I was going to rent me a fuckroom at the Bella Union and that it would cost me thirty dollars a day.

Hell. With my money from the Trust back in Rhode Island, that was no sweat.

I got myself a nice hotel room at the Alamo Hotel. One of the swankiest in town.

Then I went to the Bella Union, all decked out in the lowest-cut red dress you ever saw. I met with Mac McCready, the owner of the joint.

As soon as I'd checked out my fuckroom, I went downstairs to the bar to order myself a glass of "champagne."

I never, ever, had to pay for the glass. A horny pilgrim always appeared, paid for my wine, and agreed to my price. Anywhere from four-bits to ten bucks, depending on the quality of service he was looking for.

The services varied with the price.

For instance, some of my clients were kids who'd run away from home back East and had managed to get to Texas to become cowboys.

These ran from as young as sixteen up to about eighteen.

They were seldom very sure of themselves and would agree to pay four-bits for a hand job.

Once in the fuckroom and standing there in front of me with their pants down, they tended to be pretty shy.

I took off my clothes, let them play with my tits, and even suck the nipples while I jacked them off.

Sometimes it was all over with two or three strokes. Sometimes, if they were nervous and shivering, it took as many as ten strokes for me to get their rocks off for them.

That was a fast four-bits.

Those boys usually were return clients for as long as they were in town. And my fist got a harder and harder workout as time went on.

Pretty often they worked up to a full one-dollar fuck before they left town for the trail.

Among the more mature clients, nineteen years old and up, most just wanted a four-bit fuck. That usually lasted about seven minutes.

Some just wanted their cocks sucked. Same price. And about seven minutes, too.

About a fourth of the fellers wanted the daily-double. That's a cock sucking, but a shift to a standard fuck before he comes.

There was a price for swallowing the cum. A price for a cornhole. You can figure out the permutations of what can be done with one cock, one pair of balls, two tits, one cunt, and one ass.

The possible combinations were figured out, so they say, about the year thirty-five thousand B.C.

Now you might want to know abut the rough stuff. I'll tell you about that.

A feller who wants to beat a girl up, he has to go to a whorehouse. The madam has girls who will take that. Not a white girl, of course. Or a young one. But there are dollies, usually hopheads, who will let you beat her up for a price.

None of us independents will go for that crap.

I'll tell you a trick I had that worked fine.

What I did. I went to one of the local undertakers. And for five dollars he cut the balls off one of his stiffs and sold them to me.

I had that scrotum with balls enclosed hung up above the door inside my fuckroom. If a feller would even begin to get rough, I pointed to that bag over the door.

I'd tell him, "That's what happened to the last pilgrim tried to manhandle me."

I'd show him my stiletto and my lady pistol in the little drawer in the side table.

I've never once had so much as a tiny bruise from a client.

.....

I hung around Dallas for about six months. I loved it there. I got all the fucking and sucking I could handle between sundown and three in the morning. That's when nearly all the action takes place in a whore's day.

It was a great life for a gal who loves cock as much as I do.

And I was making at least as much money from fucking as from the stipend I got every month from the Trust.

So, I was rich, satisfied, and happy.

But I was ready to move on.

The pickings are great in a town like Dallas.

But the new towns springing up at the railroad terminals to the West were where the gold was. To say nothing of the boomtowns where miners were striking it rich. And the cattletowns where the cowboys come off the trail led by their hardons are like a cash machine.

That's where a good whore wants to be.

So, I headed West.

.....

I'd hit one bonanza after another as I moved around my Wild West.

Then, I settled down for a mite in a shithole of a settlement that was brimming with money.

It's simply called the Flat. It's near a cavalry post in West Texas called Fort Griffin.

I'd rented a fuckroom there upstairs in Shanssey's saloon. It was in that saloon that I met the one son of a bitch I fell for and will always love, Doc Holliday.

It was on September eighth, 1877, that I first saw him.

I told you I'd tell you about him.

So here goes.

Chapter Two

INTRODUCING DOC HOLLIDAY

It was just after sundown. I'd been entertaining a cowpoke in my fuckroom.

He'd come off the trail a few hours before.

He'd hit the bathhouse first. Then he'd gone to the barbershop.

Clean and shaven, he'd sauntered down to Shanssey's. He needed his wick trimmed before playing some faro.

He met me at the bar and after I'd told him my fee for the service he wanted I led him up the stairs.

When he shed his clothes and hung them up neatly, I gave him the once-over. I was already out of my own clothes by then, of course.

He was a fine specimen. Clean and smelling of bay rum from the barbershop, he had a kind of glow to his skin. The kind of shine you only see coming off blond, blond boys.

He'd sprung his hardon as soon as he'd shed his clothes. It was a beaut. It formed a bent arc. You know, so his cum hole was pointing at his bellybutton instead of out into the room. That's one of my favorite kinds of pricks. Particularly when, like his, it's thin and elegant.

What he'd told me he wanted was to get his knob polished.

His peckerhead was a pale, rose pink. I skinned back his foreskin so I could get the whole head nicely encircled with my lips.

He wanted it nice and slow. And I was only too happy to comply.

I didn't suck hard. We both wanted it to last as long as he could hold out.

My tongue played around his peephole while my lips slurped as slowly and as noisily as I could manage. I've never found a man who didn't love the sound of slurping while he's holding your head (or hair) and getting sucked nice and deep.

When the pre-cum came oozing out, I released the dong until the jism slid back inside towards his long-hanging balls.

I managed that for what must have been nearly ten or twelve minutes. He was moaning and groaning and sighing and humming and laughing. Was that cowhand ever having himself a time.

And so was I.

Finally, I ran my lips rapidly up and down over that knob. Then I swallowed deep below, sucked hard and put the boy out of his blissful misery.

As I swallowed his cum I could glance up and see his pearly white teeth as he gave me a beautiful grin.

Well, we'd both had one Hell of a time. And there at the Flat I charged four times the going rate back in Dallas.

And if you had asked either of us, we'd have to say he certainly got his money's worth.

So I washed off his gorgeous peter for him and we had both gotten dressed.

He was ready to go downstairs to gamble and I was going down to check out what kind of meat might be drifting into the saloon.

We stepped out the door onto the landing. I let my cowboy start down the stairs ahead of me.

I got about halfway down the stairs, took a look at the poker tables, and – bam!

I had never believed there was such a thing as love. I mean love of one person for another.

Oh, I knew I loved cocks. That was something else. But romantic love? I'd always thought it was hogwash.

And love at first sight? I knew absolutely that was a delusion. Lust at first sight? Sure. Happened to me all the time. And, fortunately,

I got paid for satisfying that lust.

But, as I said – bam!

As soon as I saw the thin man in the charcoal suit and the peach-colored tie, I was a goner.

When I took in those blue-gray eyes, I felt them penetrating my God damned heart.

He looked up at me, stood, smiled, took off his hat, and stole my heart.

I somehow managed to walk down the stairs without falling.

I walked right over to him.

He took my hand in his, and said, "How do you do, Ma'am. My name is Doc Holliday. I'm pleased to meet you."

He had a soft, mellifluous voice. His accent was southern and cultured. And the charm just oozed out of him.

"It's a pleasure," I said. "My name is Kate Elder. But my friends call me Big Nose Kate."

And that is how it all began.

As soon as he mentioned his name, I knew who he was.

In 1877 Doc Holliday was a national celebrity. I think I had read every article about him in the *Police Gazette* and every dime novel written with him as the protagonist in Ace Publications.

The *Police Gazette* is published in New York. Its articles about the desperados of the Wild West are written by men who have never ventured farther west than the Hudson River. The desperados they portray are such characters as Jesse James, Wild Bill Hickok, Billy the Kid, and Doc Holliday. The writing is sensational. And there is scarcely a word of truth in the so-called reporting.

Those of us living west of the Mississippi have the advantage of knowing everything written about our Western outlaws is pure bullshit.

Ace Publications issues three dime novels a week. The stories do not purport to be anything other than fiction. Among the Western heroes are Deadwood Dick, Buffalo Bill, and Doc Holliday.

Doc is portrayed as a Robin Hood character. He is described as a kindly dentist who travels the Western trails armed with a six-shooter and perfect aim. According to the stories he pulls the teeth of the needy pilgrims and Indians, robs the rich who travel by stagecoach and train, and spreads the loot among deserving homesteaders and off-their-luck miners.

In reality, the man who had arrived in the Flat was a man who was slowly wasting away from tuberculosis. He had been diagnosed with the disease five years before in Georgia and given six months to live.

He came West to drier climates, found that whiskey suppressed his cough, and was obsessed with being shot dead in a gun battle rather than rotting away in a hospital.

He became a gambler whose skillful hands enabled him to be a skilled cardshark.

In short -- Doc Holliday was my kind of man.

He invited me to join him for dinner when Shanssey's closed in the wee hours. I accepted with enthusiasm.

That evening, after we met, he played poker and won. I turned tricks and kept waiting for the early morning hours when I knew I would have Doc Holliday's dong in my hands, in my mouth, and in my cunt.

.....

When they finally closed down the saloon at 4:30 in the morning, Doc and I went to the Bon Ton Café for dinner.

I wanted to separate some fact from the fiction I had read about him. Among other things, I wanted to know how many men he had actually killed.

Doc gave me the details on his killings. He had shot a carpetbagger in Georgia after the Civil War, a man who had robbed his family of their plantation. He was suspected of the shooting but never was arrested.

After he graduated from dental college in Baltimore, and was diagnosed with his disease, he headed for Dallas. He shot two men in separate poker arguments, which caused him to become a fugitive with the Texas Rangers after him. He settled in Jacksboro, Texas, a settlement the Texas Rangers shied away from entering. Doc next shot a cavalry sergeant who was cheating at poker at his table there which put the U.S. Army on his tail. On the lam in Indian Country, he joined Ed Blanchard's gang in a train robbery and killed two passengers. He slit a man's throat in Denver.

Discounting the decapitation, Doc had earned the title of "shootist."

.....

I was fascinated by his cool telling about the men he had killed. I found it exciting. But I was even more excited by the expectation of getting that cock of his into me.

He invited me to share his bed.

For the rest of his, and my, stay in the Flat, his bed was my bed.

And let me tell you this, Pilgrims.

Doc Holliday, sick as he was physically, was the wildest fuck I ever had from any man at any time.

And coming from a woman of my experience, that says loads.

Chapter Three

TRAIL TALES

What I did with my clients up in the fuckroom, no matter whether I used my hands, mouth, or cunt, or a combination thereof, to give them professional satisfaction, could rightly be called fucking.

But what Doc and I did in our bed could only be called lovemaking.

Our lovemaking usually got started about five in the morning, after Shanssey'd locked up the saloon and Doc and I'd had buffalo or antelope or beef steak down at the Bon Ton.

Lovemaking was not a seven minute affair for Doc. That man, wasted as he appeared, and following about ten hours of constant gambling, was indefatigable.

We sucked. We fucked. We fondled. We did doggie, mom and pop, sixty-nine – every number in the book. Never for less than an hour.

Then we'd sleep until early afternoon.

Now let me tell you, that man was hung. He had the skinniest and the longest dong I've ever seen.

You know what a connoisseur of peckers I am. I thought I'd seen every size, shape, length, orientation and angle ever bestowed on a male torso.

But Doc? He was unique.

That damned thing of his, when flaccid, hung half-way down his thigh. And when it rose up in all its majesty, you would've thought he would pass out from all the blood in his brain having to rush down there to fill that fucker.

We laughed about that.

When he was shoving it to me up the cunt, he hit some sweet spots no man had ever struck before. Sent me into a cum-spasm that only Doc could give me.

Since that prick was so skinny, I could get my lips down pretty far, considering. But there was still plenty of room between my lips and his balls to get both fists around it for extra pumping while I sucked.

Despite the long dong, Doc had only normal sized balls. So how the Hell could he keep coming and coming every ten minutes or so, for an hour?

The only thing he was feeding those nuts was bourbon and rye.

Most fellers, they tie a big one on down at the bar, then come up to the fuckroom, they can't get their peckers up.

I keep the fee, of course. But I let them know that if they come back up to the room sober some other day, they get the job done for half-price.

Doc, he puts away close to a gallon of booze a day. Never wobbles, never staggers, speech never slurs, reflexes with the card deck always finely primed. And he springs a boner faster than Speedy Gonzalez.

It's the whiskey that keeps him alive. And whiskey that feeds his balls.

That's my man.

. . . . .

What Doc was, he was a tits and ass man.

Oh, he loved pussy. Don't get me wrong. But he spent more time with my tits and my ass than most fellers.

Particularly my ass.

He loved to caress it gently with that deft touch every good cardsharp has to have. He'd kiss it. He'd nuzzle it, he'd lick it. He'd talk to it.

Not the hole, mind you. Not Doc. It was my well-rounded cheeks he had a mad crush on.

One morning I asked him, "Wouldn't you like to slip that rod up the hole and see what you might find up there?"

I enjoyed taking it up the ass, of course. Ever since Rickie Dupree, when he was twelve years old and I was thirteen fumbled around and got his dick up the back alley.

There's plenty of fun to be had from that route. Trust me, if you haven't tried it.

But that wasn't for Doc.

What he answered was, "You know what I'd be likely to find up there? A piece of shit. No, thank you."

I told him I'd take an enema first if he wanted.

That appealed to him even less.

I sucked him off, and we got to talking about cornholing.

.....

"Are there many of your clients who go upstairs with you to shove it up your ass?" he asked.

I told him how it is.

The boys from the trail would never tell their stories to another male.

Absolutely.

But there are always some who will unload on us doves. So Doc had come to the right person if he wanted to hear how it is on the trail.

It's only the cowpokes just off the trail who choose to cornhole me. I've never had a paper collar, or a gambler, or a miner who chose rear entry.

Whoops! As a matter of fact, there were some miners up in Leadville... But Leadville happened later, so I couldn't tell Doc about them down on the Flat, could I?

On a cattle drive, the boys are out on the trail, a long way from poontang, for a spell of time.

They get pretty tired of abusing their grimy fists on their own hardons before long.

The young ones, sixteen to around eighteen, form their circle-jerk groups early on.

What they do, they sit back a ways from the campfire of an evening and drop their pants and chaps.

Then, they form themselves a circle and jerk each other off.

They not only like jacking off their friend to one side while getting jerked by the boy on the other side. They get a charge out of watching the others in the crowd getting off.

And there's usually some money riding on who's going to spurt into the circle first, who's jet gets closest to a target they draw on the ground beforehand, and other boy games like that.

And those boys have a name for themselves. They're called the jerks.

After eighteen, cowboys are generally too old to be invited to a circle-jerk.

Wait now. I've heard there's an exception. Cookie always gets invited, even if he's a little older. And only if he brings along a batch of lard or bacon grease. A good dab of hog-fat in the palm apparently enhances the party a great deal.

Speaking of Cookie, he's also always invited to participate with the poots.

Doc had never heard of a Poot.

The trailboys never mention them outside the drive. Poots are cowboys, just like all the rest. The difference is, they'll take it up the ass for a dollar. Most of the boys graduate from jerks to cornholers after a couple of years. And there always seem to be enough poots on the trail to keep everyone satisfied.

They are the boys who've been riding the trails and come by to see me for their favorite kind of fuck.

They are accustomed to the tight fit they get up an asshole. But they like to play with a nice pair of tits while they're getting it on. Which is where a whore comes in handy.

They come off the trail loaded with their wages. So I charge them four dollars for a cornhole.

My God, how the money rolls in.

Doc asked me if that was all that the boys had available to get their rocks off for them on the trail.

Not quite. I told him.

From what I could figure out, about one cowboy out of five out on the trail is a cocksucker.

None of them admit it. And no one responds positively to the name.

They're careful about revealing their sexual preferences. But, of course, the cocksuckers know each other from previous drives. And newcomers seem to have a way to get into the group.

Some of them prefer to suck and get sucked only by other fellers. But there are a few who, when they get to town, like a nice pair of tits and a cunt to look down on as they get their knobs polished.

And even a few who take on a daily-double.

Doc had heard all he wanted to know about the cowboys and their sex habits. He was getting sleepy, laid his head on my boobs, and fell asleep.

Chapter Four

INTRODUCING WYATT EARP

Early in December, I couldn't tell you the exact date, a big, strapping gent came into Shanssey's. He was quite an eyeful.

He stepped up to the bar and asked Harry if John Shanssey was around.

Harry told him that John was around all right. Who wanted to know?

The stranger's voice was polite, even gentle. But it was loud enough to fill the whole saloon.

"Would you let him know Wyatt Earp's in town?"

I knew the name. Everyone knew about the Earp boys.

And that Wyatt was a lawman.

He'd made a big name for himself in Wichita as a police officer for the marshal's office just two years before, in '75. The next year he moved on to Dodge City where he was appointed assistant marshal.

In both cities he'd made enough of a name for himself to get a few articles written about him in the *Police Gazette*. No dime novels yet. That would happen later. But when he arrived in the Flat in pursuit of Dave Rudabaugh, his fame had preceded him.

Harry went over to the door to John's office.

"Hey, Boss. Pilgrim out here says he's Wyatt Earp. Do you want to see him?"

John Shanssey came bursting out of his office laughing that great Irish laugh of his. He gave the stranger a tough punch to his left arm and got a resounding punch right back. The two men guffawed and gave each other bear hugs.

I guessed the two must have been pretty good friends.

Turned out I guessed right.

John took Earp back into his office and had Harry bring in a shot of Old Potrero and a glass of water.

It turned out the shot was for him, the water was for the lawman. It seemed that particular lawman did not drink booze.

Doc was in a heavy, high stakes poker game with a few of the boys at the time. He took in the whole situation without losing concentration on the deck and the pot.

I picked up the local hardware store owner and took him upstairs for a doggie style romp.

By the time we came back down the stairs, Shanssey was tending bar and the lawman was gone.

Doc's poker game broke up around two in the morning. Doc was putting the cards away and Shanssey came over to the table to talk to him. I couldn't hear what Doc and John were discussing. But it was a pretty short conversation.

. . . . .

It was after closing time, and after our morning meal at the Bon Ton, and even after our fuckfest, that I asked Doc what was going on between him and John Shanssey.

He gave me the lowdown.

. . . . .

"Did you get a load of that lawman who hit the joint late yesterday afternoon?" he asked.

"Did I see him?" I asked. "How could I miss him. He fairly made my twat twinge."

"Are you saying you found him attractive?" Doc asked.

"You'd have to ask my twat that," I teased.

"I just might do that," Doc proclaimed. "Bring that twat over here to the bed again and we'll have a close mouth to twat discussion about Marshal Wyatt Earp."

It was a while before we got back to our mouth to ear discussion.

"Seems he's a good friend of John Shanssey," Doc finally got around to telling me.

"I could tell that from the way the two greeted each other," I replied.

"You know, John was a prize fighter before he became a saloon keeper. Turns out Marshal Earp was a referee at some of those fights. They became friends back then."

"I can tell what kind of friends they must have been," I said. "The marshal always decided in John's favor."

"Probably. John won enough in the ring to bankroll buying the saloon where we work. Whatever it was, John says he owes the marshal a debt of gratitude."

"What does that have to do with you?" I asked my lover.

Doc told me what his conversation with John Shanssey was all about.

It seems that Earp had been hired by the Santa Fe Railroad to catch Dave Rudabaugh.

Rudabaugh had held up one of their trains, killed the engineer and conductor, wounded several of the passengers, and robbed close to a million dollars from the safe.

The railroad wanted Dave caught and punished. Read that "hanged."

Now Doc and I knew Dave Rudabaugh. After that heist, he'd made for the Flat.

Doc had played poker with him and won. I'd fucked him and didn't much care for him. He was a brutal fucker who slammed into my koozie with the full force of his two hundred or so pound body.

It wasn't outside the limits I set. But it was rough, gruff, and brutal.

The marshal had picked up Rudabaugh's trail, had pursued him to the Flat, and the trail turned cold.

He asked his old friend if he could dig up any information about where Dave had headed after leaving the Flat.

Shanssey didn't ask me. A desperado on the run isn't going to tell any of us whores what he's about.

But Doc was not only a gambler. He was a fellow outlaw of the local gunmen and shootists. It was a fair bet he could get a lead on where Dave Rudabaugh had headed from the Flat.

Doc was friendly with John. When he'd arrived there on the lam, John had welcomed him, befriended him, and set him up first dealing faro, and then gave him one of the poker tables to run.

But despite the fact that he liked, and owed, John, Doc turned him down.

Doc, a multiple fugitive from justice, was not inclined to help a lawman.

Well, that was that. It seemed like the end of the story. Doc and I needed some shuteye to get ready for a new day at Shanssey's.

So we fell deep asleep.

.....

The next day at sundown Doc and I got to work. Doc set up his poker table and I went to the bar to order my first glass of "champagne."

Who's the first gent to come up and offer to buy me the drink? None other than the handsome lawman himself.

I asked him what kind of entertainment he was looking for.

"I'd like a five dollar special," he told me.

I whisked him up the stairs. I could tell that there was potential here of making a haul a Hell of a lot richer than five dollars.

We got up to my fuckroom and got out of our duds.

The marshal looked real good nude. Broad chest. Bulging muscles. A handsome ass. And a cock that wasn't all that big. But back in Providence I'd gone to the museum more than once to look over those statues of the Greek gods. I was particularly impressed by the peter the sculptor had hung on Mercury. Not humungous by any means. But just plain beautiful.

Marshal Wyatt Earp's dong was just as I remembered Mercury's.

I pulled him to me and took that beaut in my mouth. I brought it up to where I could taste the pre-cum.

Then I laid down and he fucked me.

It was not a great fuck. Not by any means or measure. Just kind of unimaginative and pedestrian.

After he'd come and I'd faked an orgasm, we sat next to each other on the edge of the bed. He fondled my tits and I kept my right hand cupped over that godlike cock and those adorable balls that hung below them.

"All right, Marshal," I told him. "That was nice. Real nice. But that's not what the five dollars you gave me was for, was it?"

"Oh, that was certainly a good fuck," he assured me. "And it would ordinarily run for not much more than a dollar or a dollar and a half. But, to be honest, I was hoping I could buy your help in a little matter I rode into town for."

He told me about his meeting with John Shanssey. And how John had introduced him to Doc. And how Doc had turned him down flat.

"The Santa Fe is willing to pay very well to punish Dave Rudabaugh," he told me.

"John told me you are very good friends with Doctor Holliday. If you could manage to get the doctor to cooperate with me, I think the railroad would see clear to make it very much worth your while."

I told the marshal he'd piqued my interest. And for him to come back to the saloon the next day for another five dollar special.

Chapter Five

A DEAL WITH A LAWMAN

After the saloon closed that night, I had planned out what I would tell Doc.

We were finishing our bourbon laced coffee when I told him about my special five buck fuck with the marshal.

"Listen to what the lawman was saying again, Doc," I emphasized. "'The Santa Fe is willing to pay very well to punish Dave Rudabaugh.'"

I told Doc the amount of money I thought we could extract from the Santa Fe Railroad for a very little information about a fat ignoramus who couldn't gamble or fuck for shit.

I had his attention.

"The only way for it to work," I said. "Is to split the moolah three ways, among you, me, and John Shanssey. Neither you nor John is to give the necessary information to the marshal. As far as anyone is to know, I got the information from Rudabaugh myself when he was fucking me."

Doc liked the idea. He knew he could find out where Dave was heading and even more likely where he was staying. The Flat underworld had no love for Rudabaugh. Just by listening to his fellow desperados at the poker table, without prying, it would be as easy as...pulling teeth.

.....

The next afternoon, I had barely had time to order my "champagne" when Marshal Earp approached the bar and paid for my drink. Which, as usual, I did not drink.

I accepted his offer of five dollars for my daily special, and we headed up the steps.

I wasn't going to tell him my deal until I had entertained him with the promised joyride. I wanted to enjoy the esthetic experience of gazing fondly at that Mercurial dick. I wanted it in my hands and mouth again.

Don't forget, Ladies and Gentleman, that I am a well-educated, cultured New England lady. A graduate of a distinguished ladies' finishing school.

I considered Wyatt Earp's dong to be as culturally stimulating as one of my favorite poems by Thomas Lodge, *Rosalind*. "Love in my bosom like a bee, Doth suck his sweet."

And "suck his sweet" I did.

Bringing that lawman's prick up to near eruption, driving the jism, then back down into his balls. Crescendo up. Diminuendo down. Up, down, up, down.

God, but it's wonderful to be so cultured.

This time I was going to do it all with mouth and hand music.

When I finally let him come, the "sweet" shot into my awaiting mouth to be savored by my sensitive taste buds.

When Wyatt (I felt we were familiar enough by now to be on a first name basis) was able to settle down and discuss matters again (even with my hand still caressing that precious peter), I told him what I had to offer.

I said that it might take me a few days to give him the information. But when I felt comfortable doing so, I would be wearing a purple velvet dress when sitting at Shanssey's bar.

He would negotiate for the five dollar special. And up in the fuckroom I would tell him where Dave had headed, and probably even exactly where he was holed up.

To his credit, Wyatt did not gasp or blanch when I told him the amount we wanted from the Santa Fe Railroad Company for the information.

The money was to be delivered to me personally only if and when Wyatt Earp had apprehended Dave Rudabaugh and brought him to justice.

I, of course, named a price twice the amount I expected the railroad to agree to.

I am, you see, somewhat of a businesswoman.

Wyatt assured me that he would contact the company the next day with my offer.

.....

Doc, John, and I met in John's office the following afternoon. If we agreed to a three-way split, Doc would feel his obligation to John taken care of. John, in turn, would feel his obligation to Wyatt taken care of. And I would be receiving a very hefty sum for very little output.

.....

Doc did manage to find out, by subtle questions and judicious listening, that Dave was holed up with his gang in a ranch about twenty miles out of Fort Davies, a cavalry post right there in Texas, west of the Pecos.

The next evening, I wore my purple dress to work.

.....

There was no doubt that Wyatt had kept an eye on Shanssey's bar. Because no sooner had I plunked my ass down on the barstool than a familiar voice resounded behind me.

"May I buy the lady her glass of champagne?"

I answered, "How kind of you, Marshal Earp."

We immediately negotiated the five dollar special. To outward appearances, the marshal was merely a repeat customer for the favors of an expensive whore.

Three visits in one week for something as expensive as a five dollar fuck?

Anyone paying attention would have gathered that the lady had something pretty special to deliver.

How right that person would be.

.....

Once I had Wyatt and myself naked in my fuckroom, I marveled anew at that esthetically pleasing prick. Much better on a live torso than on a marble statue, let me tell you.

I figured, wrongly as it turned out, that this would be my last chance ever to worship that divine phallus. I wanted to enjoy just handling it, for as long as possible, with loving attention.

I had Wyatt lie down on the bed. He didn't yet have a full hardon.

I filled each of my hands with my hand crème that I keep especially for handjobs and cornholes.

With soft caresses to his balls and to his rising cock I administered the lightest massage imaginable. It was even gentler than the servicing I give to the cowhands.

I kept that lawman in a state of bliss for well nigh on to a quarter of an hour. He was in Heaven and expressed his euphoria with soft coos that would have surprised the recipients of the buffalos [1] he had administered so famously on rowdy citizens in Wichita and Dodge.

But, if he was in Heaven, I was more so. Gently playing with that divine turgid cock was, for me, more like praying than any activity I had participated in at the churches my parents had dragged me to in my youth.

When his cock finally gave that tell-tale twitch that indicted he was about to come, I circled that rosy pink bulb with my lips and sucked his cum worshipfully into my mouth and throat.

It's a moment I shall never forget.

.....

When we had both recovered, it was time to talk turkey.

I told Wyatt that I had the information he wanted and would give it to him if the railroad was willing to pay for it.

It was my turn to be surprised. The Santa Fe Railroad had such a hardon for Dave Rudabaugh they were willing to pay me the full price I had asked.

1 Buffalo: Wyatt Earp was famous for buffaloing miscreants rather than shooting them. A "buffalo" was a pistol whip to the head of the perpetrator.

As you know, Doc, John, and I would have been content with half the amount.

"Then we have a deal," I told Wyatt. "No need to sign a contract. I know your word is better than any damned piece of paper."

"I appreciate that, Kate," he said.

"I'll expect the reward money here in my hand as soon as you can get here for a five dollar special after delivering Dave Rudabaugh, dead or alive, to the people who hired you."

We shook hands. And I realized that I was wrong when I thought I'd had my last rendezvous with the cock I adored.

The money I would be receiving was fine. I could always use more cash. But, truth to tell, the prospect of getting that cock in my hands, in my mouth, or up my snatch again gave me a much warmer feeling.

I told Wyatt where he could find his prey.

I followed him out the door and down the stairs to the saloon.

As he went out onto the street and mounted his horse, he didn't so much as say goodbye.

We both knew we should be seen as just another whore and her client.

No one could tell that my heart was beating faster as he rode off.

.....

Two weeks went by. We didn't hear a word from Wyatt Earp.

We didn't expect to. No one wanted the word to get out to anyone, anywhere, that we had sold Dave Rudabaugh for a very hefty sum.

Nobody's damned business but our own.

.....

News spread around the entire West, and spilled over to the East by an article in the *Police Gazette*, that Wyatt Earp, the hero of Wichita and Dodge City, had tracked down the vile desperado, Dave Rudabaugh, and his entire gang.

The public knew there had been a shootout between the marshal and his posse and the villain and his gang near a distant military outpost somewhere west of the Pecos River.

Wyatt himself had shot Dave dead and sent his body, COD, to the headquarters of the railroad in Topeka, Kansas.

. . . . .

When Earp came riding into the Flat after that exploit, it was as a true celebrity. A hero to some, a villain to others.

It depended on which side of the law you were rooting for.

But, he was definitely a celebrity.

. . . . .

He did not come directly to Shanssey's. None of us wanted his name connected directly to us.

He gambled and whored at several saloons over the next week or so.

When he finally came moseying into Shanssey's he brought his saddle bags in with him.

No one could have guessed what was in those innocent looking bags.

He stopped at the bar, bought me a glass of "champagne," and negotiated a five dollar special.

He carried his saddlebags up the stairs with him.

I did not choose to look into those bags first.

What I was eagerly waiting to see were the cock and balls I'd been dreaming about and waiting for ever since he'd left the Flat a few weeks before.

The marshal clearly had decided he was quite fond of the five dollar special.

So, before dealing with the reward money, we took care of getting out of our clothes.

This time, our sex experience was different.

Before, I had serviced Wyatt, and he had passively, but joyfully, succumbed to the loving attention I had given to his peter.

This time, he chose to be the seducer.

Well, it doesn't take much to seduce a whore. We are sure things. That's what we get paid for.

But, while I kept a sure grip on those treasures that thrust up and hung down from his crotch, he spent over a half-hour kissing my mouth, sucking my tits, and licking my cunt.

As this was going on, I kept caressing his dick and balls. But I knew he would want to come inside my pussy this time. So I kept the caresses as gentle as I could.

Once he was ready to fuck, he mounted me.

As before, it was a pretty unimaginative performance.

But I have to admit. Feeling that boner that I worshipped spurting its jism up my hole was a real treat – even at the end of a pretty tepid set of thrusts.

.....

It was time then for him to hand over the money he owed us. I didn't count out the bills. I knew he was good for it.

Even though I'd earned it, I couldn't help but say "Thank you, Wyatt."

"Nothing to thank me for," he replied politely. "You are the one who helped me. Dave's trail had grown cold, and I doubt I would've ever picked it up.

"Believe me, Kate, you always have a friend in Wyatt Earp. If you and Doc ever get over Dodge way, you're likely to find me there. And the welcome mat will always be out."

.....

When Shanssey closed up for the night, Doc and I stayed inside with him.

John and Doc went into John's office.

I went upstairs and brought down the loot.

We split it as agreed, three ways.

John had a bottle of Old Crow open, and we killed that bottle, toasting what Doc called a "nifty haul."

When I told the two what Wyatt had said to me, John assured us.

"Believe me, you two. When Wyatt Earp tells you he's your friend, you've got a friend for life. No matter what, if he thinks he owes you, he'll always be on your side."

I put that marker away in my mind.
And I later found that what John had said was absolutely true.

Chapter Six

ESCAPE FROM A HANGING

Wyatt stayed in the Flat for a while after delivering the money to us. By unspoken agreement he kept his distance from John, Doc, and me. He continued to gamble and whore all over the settlement and dropped by Shanssey's only once, and that was to buck the tiger at Lottie Deno's faro bank.

He did not even nod a greeting to his three collaborators in the capture of Dave Rudabaugh.

. . . . .

One evening, Ed Bailey came to Shanssey's to play some poker.

Ed was quite a man abut town. He was an active trader in buffalo hides and in horse trading. He had been a resident of the Flat for long enough to be considered a "local."

He was respected in certain circles as a leader of the vigilante committee.

Quite a man to be reckoned with.

Ed was sure of his gun and unafraid of getting into a fight. The sort of man who might intimidate the timid.

He sat down at a poker table with Doc.

As you know, Doc was the last man ever to be considered timid.

In addition to Doc and Ed Bailey, there were four other players at the table. It was a high stakes game and was quite lively.

The game was straight five card draw, Jacks or better to open.

Doc later told me how the fracas at his table got started.

Ed kept sneaking looks at the deadwood.[2]

The practice is clearly cheating and is not allowed by the gambling rules anywhere.

The protocol is that if a player is caught sneaking peeks at the deadwood he loses the pot.

Doc caught Ed at it and warned him saying, "Play poker, Ed."

I was just coming down the stairs with a young client who had just received my four-bit jack off.

He was smiling, relieved and happy.

I heard Doc's tone of voice downstairs and decided to walk back up to the landing to see what was going on.

I saw Ed trying to glimpse at the deadwood again. It was clear what was up.

As Ed's hands touched the pile of cards, Doc pulled down the pot without showing his hand.

Bailey drew his gun.

Doc was in a position at the table where he couldn't outdraw Ed. He was sitting right next to him, though.

In addition to his two six-shooters, Doc had a razor-sharp knife located in a sheath up his coat-sleeve. It was spring-loaded, so that it could drop into his awaiting hand in a split second.

The moment the stiletto hit Doc's hand, he inserted it right into Ed's heart.

Everyone at the table had seen the entire action.

And in addition, there were many of us who were not at the table who observed that Ed had drawn first on Doc. And that Doc had reacted in self-defense.

Doc knew he was in the right. And when the town marshal, Rob Bixby, arrived, he submitted to arrest. Doc knew that in an open-and-

2 Deadwood: The discard pile of cards in the game of five card draw. Seeing what your opponents have discarded gives an advantage to a player.

shut case of self-defense, any court in the West would acquit him.

Ed's body was still seeping blood onto the baize covered table as Doc left the saloon under the custody of Bixby and two of his deputy marshals.

I was witness to the whole proceeding, but remained on the landing to observe what would happen next.

In the saloon there were several members of Bailey's vigilante group.

Their leader lay sprawled out on a table, killed by a man known as a killer.

I could see the vigilantes run out of Shanssey's. It was clear they were heading out to gather their fellow members to serve vigilante justice on the man who had "murdered" their leader.

Before Bixby and his boys could get Doc to the local jail, the lynch crowd was on its way to grab Doc away from the marshal and his men.

The lawmen whisked Doc into the Lone Star Hotel to protect him.

I knew the three local lawmen could not hold off the angry crowd for long. That crowd was intent on hanging Doc and could certainly get past the marshal and his deputies, given time.

I circled around to the back of the hotel. Some of the vigilantes had already gathered there to obstruct any escape by the back door.

At the back of the lot occupied by the hotel there was a wooden shack.

I checked it out and saw that a horse was stabled there, and that the shack was loaded with hay.

It was time for quick action by Big Nose Kate.

I had to get that horse out of that shack, find two getaway horses, gather our money and some belongings, cause a distraction, and get Doc and me away from that angry crowd that was gathered to hang my man. And I didn't have long to do all that.

The Griffin Arms Hotel was close by. I knew Wyatt was there.

I ran in and up to his room and in a few words apprised him of the situation.

I sent him to get the horse out of the shed.

He shot out of his room like a cannon ball.

Next I got to our hotel and got our cash and as much of our essentials as I could into two saddlebags.

Next I "liberated" two ponies from the hotel's stable, threw on saddles and saddlebags and rode like Hell back to that shack behind the Lone Star.

In passing, I noticed that the crowd outside the hotel was growing more restless and hostile.

I galloped behind the hotel and saw that Wyatt had rescued the horse from it.

I set fire to the shed and got out of there in a jiffy.

The whole settlement of the Flat was a tinderbox. Everyone living there knew that fire was the worst enemy the town could face. It could burn the settlement off the face of the earth, if not in seconds, in minutes.

As soon as the fire flared up, everyone who had been swarming in front of the hotel forgot everything and rushed to put out the fire before it burned down the town.

The way was now clear for me.

I rushed into the hotel, drew a bead on Bixby and his boys, and threw a pistol to Doc.

Doc disarmed the lawmen, and together he and I rushed out to mount the awaiting ponies.

And while the whole town was busy putting out the threatening fire, Doc and I were headed out of town.

We knew where we were headed. Dodge City was four hundred miles away. Wyatt Earp, our new friend would be heading home to Dodge eventually. We were sure of that.

. . . . .

I had saved Doc's ass from an angry lynch mob. In other words, I now had Doctor John Henry Holliday by the balls.

We never discussed his obligation to me. We didn't have to. We both understood it.

The code of honor shared by both Wyatt Earp, lawman, and Doc Holliday, outlaw, was irrevocable. A man, once indebted, must always pay his debts.

By that code, I was, forever more, Doc Holliday's woman. And under my conditions, not his.

Although he was my man, I could love him or leave him.

Again, he was bound to me. I was not bound to him.

And with that understanding, we rode four hundred miles through hostile Indian country, to live as best we could under harsh conditions, until we could make it to Dodge City, Kansas.

Chapter Seven

A PROPER COUPLE

Why did we choose Dodge City as our destination?

Easy.

Because it was Wyatt Earp's headquarters. And come Hell or high water, from then on, Wyatt was our friend.

Earp had helped us by getting the horse out of the shack. Doc owed him one for that. His Southern Code meant that he was indebted to Wyatt Earp. He owed him loyalty. In short, Doc had a friend. Other than me, of course.

Doc was the most moral man I ever knew. You might think that a man who was a bloodthirsty murderer, an unprincipled confidence man, and an unscrupulous liar and cheat, was immoral.

You would be wrong.

The code he lived by was the one he was born to as a Georgian, as a son of the Old South.

He was a gentleman. And it was instilled in his soul that a gentleman always pays his debts.

He owed Wyatt Earp for helping him with the horse in his hour of need. He owed him loyalty.

The flight from Fort Griffin to Dodge was long, tough, and cold. It was winter. The nights were cold, and we traveled without shelter or blankets. The trail was through Indian Territory, patrolled by wild Comanches, Cheyennes, and Cherokees. It was a hideout for desperados like us who would plug you for a nickel and laugh. Food and lodging were not for sale.

We camped under the stars. We shot or gathered our food and cooked it as best we could. The only entertainment for us as we fled over that wasteland was fucking. Fucking kept us happy. Fucking kept us warm. And fucking kept us from wondering if there was a Comanche lurking in the night looking to slit our throats or rape me, or both.

It was a happy hour when we finally made it to Dodge.

We did not come into Dodge with many belongings. But one thing we *did* have. We were loaded with money from the deal with Wyatt and the Santa Fe Railroad.

We bought ourselves the finest duds available. We ate at the finest hash houses in town. And we took deluxe rooms at Deacon Cox's boardinghouse as Doctor and Missus John Henry Holliday.

Not that any preacherman had joined us in holy matrimony. Doc's personal code was what made us man and wife for better or worse. And some of our life together was for the better, of course. But a Hell of a lot of it was for worse, too.

There we were, Doc and me, in December 1877, living high and mighty in Dodge City, Kansas. And Doc, the fucking idiot, got it into his head he was going to do me the great favor of making me genteel. Hell, my folks had tried that when I was young and more malleable. But, to keep him happy for a while, I went along with the fucking deal.

But if he thought Big Nose Kate was going to give up whoring, he had another think coming. Then, as now, I loved cock and I loved getting paid for fucking and sucking it. Nothing in this God damned world will ever change that.

By Doc's code he was married to me. I sure as Hell wasn't married to him.

Doc figured that if he was to make me respectable, he had to get respectable himself.

There was no other dentist in Dodge, so he hung up his shingle.

.....

Well, Doc was dentisting. And we attended all the shows in town. And there was plenty of theater to keep the town entertained. There was more money circulating in Dodge City at the time than in any city in the country. We got Eddie Foy, the comedian. We got Lily Langtree, the singer. And Lola Montez the dancer.

We got Shakespearian actors doing Shakespeare. We got musical comedy stars doing musical comedy. We got can-can dancers from Paris and hootchy-kootchy dancers from God knows where.

We had oysters from New York, lobsters from Maine, and crabs from Maryland.

We had beef, cooked every way you can imagine.

Lamb? Not so much. In a cattleman's town like Dodge, you've got to be carrying heavy weaponry with you if you have the balls to order lamb chops at an eatery.

So we kept ourselves properly entertained in the evenings.

.....

But when Doc was off pulling teeth during the day, what was I supposed to be doing to fill in the time?

Well, for one thing, I fucked the landlord a lot. Deacon Cox wasn't getting much from his missus. His nuts needed discharging big time. And my cunt was waiting.

There were delivery boys and the mailman who came by the boardinghouse. They made their deliveries. And I delivered.

Before you knew it, we were up to our asses in deliveries.

Word tended to get around that Missus John Henry Holliday had a hot twat.

I didn't keep what we cultured people call our "liaisons" secret from Doc.

I'd tell him about how I sometimes had to help our landlord get it up. I told him the mailman had a wart on his dick. (He didn't, but I loved to rattle Doc's cage.) I told him that the boy who delivered the newspaper always stopped by my room to get his peter jacked off by the nice lady who was married to the dentist.

(As a matter of fact, that happened to be the truth.)

I'd tell Doc stuff that happened and things that I'd just make up to show him that nobody, not even the man who claimed to be my husband, can decide what Kate Elder can and cannot do.

When we fought, it often got physical. There was an unstated rule that we would not bruise each other's faces. Doc, as a society dentist, did not need to sport a black eye.

I, as a proper member of the town's gentry, and also, a lady who enjoyed the company of assorted visitors, did not need a bruised cheek.

But we did punch. And we did pinch.

But most of all we fucked with that fierceness I had first fallen in love with the first night we met and Doc screwed the Hell out of me.

All our fights ended up with mad fucking.

Enough to wear a poor girl out.

I loved it.

.....

Doc finally had to come to the realization that he wasn't going to make a "lady" out of me. My parents hadn't ben able to. Miss Claybourne hadn't been able to.

No one was going to make Katherine Elder into anything other than Big Nose Kate, the happy whore.

.....

Even though he was the only dentist in town, Doc's practice wasn't exactly thriving.

It turned out that most people in town had to have a pretty severe dental problem to allow a consumptive dentist, who coughed up blood while in their face, to extract a tooth.

So Doc opened shop less and less frequently.

And he relaxed into acceptance of who I was.

I wasn't really whoring again. Doc's hours at his dental practice meant he and I were out on the town in the evenings. So I had to content myself with my daytime *liaisons*.

I'll tell you about one evening we had when Doc was beginning to mellow out quite a bit.

.....

We got all dressed up in our fancy clothes, and visited the Alhambra Saloon with the intent of doing some drinking and gambling.

I had been considering which saloon in town I'd choose where I could sell my ass when Doc got back to his senses. I knew it wouldn't be long now before he decided to give up pulling teeth and become a gambler and possibly an outlaw again.

I liked the look of the Alhambra as we stepped in the door. You know how you just feel comfortable in some places immediately? It was like that.

I decided on the spot that this place was for me.

As we were heading for the bar to get in some serious drinking, we passed by a table of drunk cowhands.

"Have a snort," said a brash asshole.

"Oh, no," says Doc, real prim like. "We're teetotalers."

"Come on," the asshole insisted. "It's time you tried it."

I took a look at Doc. The smile on his face told me quite clearly that he intended to exercise his skill as a confidence man.

I was ready to get a kick out of what was about to happen to the asshole cowhand without knowing just what kind of prank Doc would play on him.

The asshole filled two glasses from the bottle of Old Potrero on his table, drew his gun, and pointed it at Doc.

"Down the hatch, you two," the cowboy snarled.

His friends began to snigger at the two of us, being forced to drink for their amusement.

"I regret to say, Sir, that liquor has never touched our lips," Doc said. "You see, we are a good Christian couple, and come from firm teetotaler families."

"My pistol here says you two tee totaling fuckers are going to down some of this hooch right now. While we watch" the jerkoff laughed.

"Oh, dear," Doc whimpered. "What would daddy say?"

I was onto his con and said, "He'd be so disappointed."

I looked at the drawn gun and shivered.

"Well," I said in a frightened voice. "Considering that this big, strong, manly cowboy might hurt us if we don't take a sip, I guess we'll have to throw scruples aside."

The asshole thrust the glasses, filled with our favorite rye whiskey, at us.

"Drink it down. Every fucking drop," the prick said.

Oh, we guzzled it down, making pained expressions.

The drunk cowboys laughed their asses off.

The brash leader was guffawing something fierce He grabbed the glasses and filled them again. Used up damn near half a bottle. He was having himself a grand old time enjoying the misery of making the teetotalers drink booze.

Still protesting, Doc and I finished off the whole bottle, except for a tiny bit in the bottom.

Doc threw the remainder of the drink in the cowboy's face, grabbed the amazed cowboy's gun, slipped it in his own pocket, and we walked away with the cowhand's laughing at their buddy.

The one who'd been harassing us got up from the table and came lurching at us.

Doc pointed the pistol he'd taken from him, pointed it directly between his eyes and said, "One more step, Cowboy, and I will have to defend myself by blowing your fucking brains out."

The cowboy sobered up real quick. The steady, deadly look in Doc's eyes told him all he needed to know.

The game was over.

.....

When I told Doc I had made my mind up to rent a fuckroom at the Alhambra, he fairly seethed. We had a rip-roaring old fight and fuck about it.

But he'd softened up in his feelings about me fucking everyone who happened to come to Deacon Cox's boardinghouse. So he finally gave in.

I had told him I only fucked those who struck my fancy.

(All right. I have to admit nearly every male with a prick between his legs caught my fancy. You know how I am about pricks.)

And Doc knew his dentistry days in Dodge would soon come to a crashing end. And that his dream of being a righteous, pious appearing medical man would succumb to his real talents – gambling and killing.

But it was hard for him to give up his stupid dream of making me into a respectable lady. At least in the eyes of the world.

What I did in our bedroom when he was away – he felt he could live with that.

.....

I figured out the unbelievable way Doc felt about my life as a fully practicing professional whore.

It went like this.

I had saved his life. True.

He was then, under an obligation to me. Not true.

I hadn't saved him from the lynch mob for him to be indebted to me. I had saved him because he and I were friends and lovers. And because he had that long, long superpeter that hit me in all the right places.

I had loved him back at the Flat because he accepted me for exactly what I was and am. A pecker-obsessed whore who loves to fuck and suck.

Now, to "pay me back" for what I had done for him, he had to reward me by freeing me from a life of "sin and depravity."

Bullshit!

After a week or so of verbal and physical fighting, and of brutal fucking, he gave in.

He felt he was obligated to me.

I never felt obligated to anyone, ever, including John Henry Holliday, D.D.S.

It all ended with Doc hauling down his shingle at his dental office and seating himself at a poker table at the Alhambra armed with two pistols and a stiletto.

Yes, at the Alhambra where I had already set up my own practice in an upstairs fuckroom.

.....

God, the pleasures and surprises I encountered in that room.

I fondly remember a time there at the Alhambra when I agreed to take a young virgin cowpoke up to my fuckroom for just two-bits.

He assured me that was all he had left, having blown his entire wages bucking the tiger at faro.

He was a really cute kid. Good looking, shy, sweet smile. He wanted so to lose his cherry.

So, why not, this one time, be a two-bit whore?

Once we got nude in the fuckroom, the poor kid was too nervous to get it up. He began to shake and I saw he was going to cry.

So I fondled his cock and balls. I sucked his young cock, making those slurping noises fellers love so. Then I ran an oiled finger up his asshole and gently massaged his prostate gland.

As his pecker jetted up, I gave it the old bulb squeeze with my lips and sucked the jism right up from the bottom of his ball-sack.

The youngster gave me a shy smile and said, ""Thank you, Ma'am."

I answered, "You're welcome, Buster. Come back and see me sometime when you can rustle up another two-bits."

He managed to borrow a few quarters from his pals over the next few days before he had to hit the trail again.

And he told me he spent it all on return engagements to my upstairs room.

It made me feel like some kind of God damned saint for what I'd done for that boy.

.....

Here's another Alhambra memory that keeps popping into my head still.

I was at the bar there, ordering my "champagne" when a youthful voice behind me asked, "May I be so bold as to buy the lady a drink?"

"A real gentleman," I think to myself. "And from the voice, I would guess a sweet, juicy young one."

Before turning around to acknowledge the offer, I pictured a delicious, fragrant youthful cock in my mouth. Yep, I could practically taste it. No matter what the young pilgrim might want in the way of servicing, I was going to give that callow cock a good tasting.

I turned around to accept the offer and was practically swept off my feet.

Smiling at me was one of the most handsome prospective clients I had ever laid eyes on.

Pale skinned and blond. Certainly not a trailhand. This hunk of gorgeous had not ever spent much time out in the Kansas or Texas sun.

Clear -- I suppose you could almost say limpid – blue eyes that just melted my heart. Slender, not skinny.

Well, I could go on and on.

"Thank you, Stranger," I said. "Are you looking for a little sport? A good time?"

"You've got that right, Lady," was the answer.

"My name's Kate," I said. "What's yours? And what kind of sport are you thinking of?"

It turned out that what the stranger was looking for was something somewhat more exotic than a four-bit fuck. I was content to work out the details when we would get up to the fuckroom.

I set the price at a buck.

That turned out to be agreeable.

Hell, to get my lips around what I was sure to be prime, A-1 meat, I would do just about anything the youth was looking for.

We got up the stairs and into the room where I stashed the silver dollar in my lockbox.

Before disrobing, I reached down to get a feel of the tool that resided within my client's britches.

Not much there.

But with the young ones, I'd early on discovered that the cocks are very supple when still soft. And if I do say so, very pretty.

I love to tease up a flaccid sixteen to eighteen year old smallish to medium sized peter. I get my hands, pre-oiled, slithering around that little hooded sausage and those discretely hanging nuts. I then coax the shebang into a peek-a-boo state that I slide into my drooling mouth.

We got out of our clothes, and what's the first thing I see?

My client's got tits.

Well, more titties than tits I'd have to call them. Not too much larger than a couple of fried eggs. But definitely bosoms.

My eye slides down to behold a blond triangular bush pointing directly to a …? What's that I spy?

It's a cunt.

Now, as you know, I like cunts a lot. Not anywhere near as much as cocks. But nuzzling down there where I can get a good whiff of that sweet, ocean-scented pussy and lick around until I can suck a clit and get a finger up a hole, and then follow up with licking those lower lips?

Heavenly!

I have always found that life is quite lovely in that garden of delights.

I started to go down on the young lady.

But whoa! That's not what she wanted.

Out of the totebag she'd brought up was a strap she fastened around her midsection.

Next, she pulled out a dildo.

This one had little bumps and hollows carved up and down it. The pole was made of ivory and the bulb at the top was larger than you'd find on a normal male and was soft, spongy kind of fuzzy.

She slipped the dildo into the receptacle in the strap and got a handful of the hand crème I keep available all the time on the side table.

I looked at that dildo and already missed that mouthful of young male cock I had been planning to enjoy.

But, what the Hell! A whore gets what she gets in the way of peters. And this dildo promised to give a new kind of thrill.

And I looked forward to playing with and sucking those cute little titties.

Well, Sir. She fucked me in the cunt. She fucked me up the ass. She fondled, kissed, and sucked my tits. She was great giving mouth music to my cunt.

In short, she gave me a real royal treatment.

Then she put the strap on me and inserted the dildo.

I fucked her in the cunt. I told her to suck the dildo which was now delightfully cunt-flavored. I gave it to her up the ass.

I sucked her tits until those nipples had changed from rosy pink to blood red.

By the time she'd finished with me and I'd finished with her, I certainly could not regret the lost chance to suck teen-age cock that evening.

During the month's stay I had whoring at the Alhambra, I had enjoyed gorging on cock of all kinds.

But that one time, with the girl with the strap turned out to be a memory to keep up there with the more precious recollections.

. . . . .

Not long after I'd had my lesbian client, Wyatt arrived in Dodge.

He'd been away chasing the James Brothers and their gang all over Kansas, Nebraska, Missouri, and Indian Territory.

The James Boys dodged him again and again.

The pursuit was turning out to be downright unprofitable, so he came back to his headquarters in Dodge.

We had a joyful reunion.

. . . . .

Well, with Wyatt in town, we had us a friend who knew us for who we were and accepted us for who we were.

Wyatt, Doc, and Big Nose Kate. Weren't we a threesome, though!

Of an evening we took in the town regular.

We visited every saloon in town. Doc and I had what Doc called our cocktails and Wyatt drank something called nearbeer.

We visited the gambling hells where Doc and Wyatt played poker and I bucked the tiger at the faro bank.

Theater? We all three loved it. Everything from girly shows to Shakespeare.

It was a grand time.

When we weren't gadding around with Wyatt, Doc was at his table at the Alhambra and I was fucking the boys in my fuckroom upstairs.

Of course, I didn't fuck either Doc or Wyatt in the fuckroom.

Doc and I fucked like a couple of wildcats still in our bed at the deacon's. And I fucked Wyatt in his room over at the Longhorn Hotel.

Doc knew I was fucking Wyatt. And Wyatt knew Doc knew.

I still worshipped, and will always worship Wyatt Earp's dong.

And it was crystal clear that Wyatt was crazy about having his prick worshipped with such enthusiasm.

Surely Doc could understand that. Couldn't he?

I even told Doc that his friend Wyatt was a better fuck than him. That wasn't the truth, of course. I only did it for pure bitchiness.

But even though I was fucking both Doc and Wyatt, that didn't change the fact that my two lovers were fast friends.

I don't see anything peculiar in that.

Do you?

Chapter Eight

LEADVILLE SOJOURN

We were happy enough in Dodge. But as the months rolled by, both Doc and I felt we were in a kind of a rut. We had never been fixed in one place very long once we'd come West.

Wyatt had been appointed Deputy Marshal again in Dodge City, and had begun to pal around more and more with the Masterson brothers.

Doc and Bat Masterson never hit it off very well with each other.

So, although Doc was still beholden to Wyatt, and I still loved that man's dick, we began to yearn for a bit of adventure.

In the spring of 1878, there were some fabulous silver strikes in Leadville, Colorado.

From everything we'd heard, the area was swarming with young miners. These were the boys who had been too young to get in on the former gold and silver rushes and aimed to get rich in Leadville.

Word was that very few professional gamblers had moved in on the pickings yet. And I'd heard that Leadville was a town with not a single whore and hundreds of newly rich miners.

The downside of considering going there was that Leadville is two miles high up in the Rockies. And Doc's lungs had stood up years past what his doctor back in Georgia had predicted possible. But recently he had begun to cough up lots and lots of blood. More than he had ever bled before.

I wasn't so sure he should put those lungs to the test of a place where the oxygen is pretty damned thin.

But Doc pooh-poohed the health risk. He was restless and ready to play cards with the newly rich young miners.

And I was hot to get my mouth and twat around the fresh young meat of the far-west boys.

So, we told Wyatt we'd return to Dodge when we'd squeezed as much silver as we could carry back from the Colorado Rockies. We got ourselves on the road to Leadville by means of three train rides and a journey by stagecoach.

.....

When we got to Leadville, the "town" made the Flat look like Paradise.

Flimsy buildings had been slapped together out of ripsawed timber, bare logs, and mud.

But as primitive as the fabrication was of the buildings, there were three banks, a hardware store, an assayer's office, four hotels, ten saloons, a swarm of hotbed hostelries, a bunch of tiny beaneries all run by Chinese, and three stables.

And yet, with all those amenities, there was not a whorehouse or even an independent like me in town.

All the saloons had gambling tables, and Doc discovered that some professional gamblers had beaten him up to the digs. But he was the only major player on the professional gambling circuit in town.

Doc took a table at the Two High Saloon. But his cough got him to hacking up blood something awful and he could hardly eat a bite. Bourbon and rye had always helped him control his disease before. He increased his guzzling to more booze than any one human should be able to get down without falling on his fucking face.

But to no avail.

There was no way he could brook the kind of hours at a poker table that a professional gambler had to stand.

Even so, he wasn't ready yet to give it all up and hightail it back to Dodge.

So, instead, he turned his talents to a complicated confidence game.

It involved taking a gullible banker from Indiana for some half a million dollars.

The banker had come to Leadville thinking there had to be ways of making a killing from the rich silver load.

Doc and a confidant concocted a scheme about a supposed stash of stolen gold bullion sunk in a near-by lake.

I couldn't possibly begin to tell you the whole complicated story.

But, in short, the banker got bilked and Doc made one Hell of a haul.

And the scam didn't play fuck-all with his expiring lungs the way gambling would have.

While Doc was working his scam, I came up with a little business proposition I figured out all by myself.

There I was, in a town swarming with rich, young, horny miners.

Those fellers needed a woman something awful.

And, as I said, there I was, Big Nose Kate, not only the best fuck in Colorado. I was the only whore in town.

I went to Ralph Snyder, the proprietor of the Silver Queen Saloon.

He hadn't been able to get a second story built yet for his booze emporium. So there were no cribs or fuckrooms in the joint.

With no whores or whoremasters in town yet, there was no need for them anyway.

What Ralph did have was a good-sized storage room in back that was only half full of supplies.

I told him that from my perspective, it looked half empty.

So I rented that half-empty space from him for a hefty fee. But I knew I could make a little fortune there, and have myself a Hell of a time while doing so.

What I set up was what I called my "four-ring circus."

I'll tell you how it worked.

When word got out, starting at sundown the boys began lining up outside the storeroom door.

I charged twenty-five dollars per head.

My God! Who ever heard of a whore getting money like that from an inexhaustible lineup of randy young men?

The clients were given to know what they could expect for their twenty-five buck entry fee to the circus.

I took in four at a time. Add that up in your head. A hundreds of dollars per performance. And no performance lasted over ten minutes.

It was all a stand-up show.

The lads were not given an opportunity to choose what part each was to play.

I passed out cards to them, one at a time.

There was a Jack of Hearts, a King of Spades, a King of Diamonds, and a King of Clubs.

Here's how it worked.

After we all got ourselves undressed, I arranged them around me.

While I was jacking off the Jack of Hearts I sucked off the King of Spades. The King of Diamonds was fucking me in the ass at the same time while the King of Clubs fucked me in the twat.

Now, you might think that an ordinary whore couldn't pull off an act like that.

You're right. Your four-bit whore couldn't.

But Big Nose Kate, a hundred dollars an hour artiste, given a mining camp full of desperate youngsters, was able to satisfy the hordes.

. . . . .

Doc pulled off his scam and was anxious to get back to Dodge and give his lungs a break.

I'd loved my circus, but I was plumb worn out.

So, having had our fill of the two-mile high camp, we hauled asses back to Dodge City.

And we were a Hell of a lot richer for our sojourn in the Rockies.

Chapter Nine

BACK TO DODGE

During the trip back to Dodge, Doc's lungs seemed to improve some. But it looked to me as though the stay in Leadville had done permanent damage to them.

He was coughing up a lot more blood than he had before. And he had gotten skinny enough to worry me.

When we got to Dodge, Wyatt was down at the train station and greeted us both like returning members of his family.

Later that day we ran into Bat Masterson and his snot-nosed brother.

They, like Wyatt, were also deputy marshals.

They gave Doc the most cold-eyed greeting I'd ever seen.

There was no love lost between the fucking Mastersons and Doc Holliday

.....

The day after we'd returned to Dodge, Doc returned to his table at the Alhambra. He bore up under the strain of the hours he sat playing poker pretty well. It took as much whiskey as he'd started to drink in Leadville to control his cough. But he wasn't driving any gamblers away from his table, from what I could see, with his sickness.

My old fuckroom was still available, so I was able to pleasure the boys with the bucks again and keep myself contented.

. . . . .

We'd been back in Dodge one month to the day when a situation occurred that changed our relationship with Wyatt.

I was fucking him again in his hotel room. Hell, I had afternoons free and he could work out times to get free from making life miserable for cowboys who came into town to get cantankerous.

Well, this one day, a big herd of cattle had been brought into Dodge. And the cowhands who had driven them up from Texas were as wild and wooly a bunch as you can imagine.

It was about eight o'clock in the evening and I had just gotten a client in my fuckroom down to his birthday suit. And I was getting out of my dress slow and seductive like.

I heard whoops and hollers outside the Alhambra, closing in on the rear entrance.

The cowhands, paid off by the cattle barons and carrying lots of cash still, were liquored up, shouting obscenities and shooting their firearms here, there, and everywhere. They were in one mean mood. You could tell.

My client started to shiver. Then he lost his hardon.

I could tell the feller was a lost cause.

I kept his money, of course. But I told him to get back into his duds. I informed him he could come back the next day and get his cock sucked for half price.

That satisfied him.

What he clearly wanted to do was get the fuck out of the saloon before the rowdy cowboys came in and started shooting the place up.

We headed out the fuckroom door and onto the landing.

He skedaddled down the stairs.

I remained up on the landing, taking a gander at what was going on down below.

The bottom floor turned dead quiet.

Most of the customers stopped doing whatever they'd been

doing and headed out the front door.

At Doc's table, there were five players. Three of them cashed in their chips and left.

Doc and Stan Billingsley, a regular player at his table, sat stock still.

Doc reached into his two holsters and retrieved his pistols.

He got up from the table and walked determinedly towards the door outside of which the hubbub had been resounding.

A voice emerged from the riotous crowd.

"Hey, boys," we heard a voice. "Lookie who we just cornered. It's that no good, pissy-anty, son of a bitch, Deputy Marshal, Wyatt Earp. The big man who buffaloed me last time we met in Wichita."

The crowd cheered.

The leader of the rowdy, drunk group was Ed Morrison. I knew him from when we were in Dodge before. And, I sure enough knew, Wyatt had indeed buffaloed him some years previous.

"Got you at last," Morrison taunted. "Say your prayers, Mister Big Shot Buffalo-a-man-just-because-he's-out-having-hisself-time. Because, Mister Earp, you ain't got more an seconds to live."

Doc, with his pistols cocked, shouted out the door, "Hey, Big Mouth out there. I've got you covered. And the rest of you, too. Drop your guns before I count to three or you'll all be deadmen starting with Mister Big Mouth Asshole."

Every member of the group, including Morrison of course, dropped their guns and high-tailed it back out of town.

. . . . .

When the crowd had fully dispersed outside, Wyatt walked into the saloon and shook hands with Doc.

"Thanks, Pard. I reckon you saved my life. I owe you one."

"Forget about it," Doc answered. "No more than you would've done for me."

I came down the stairs.

Wyatt came over to me.

"That's one Hell of a man you've got there," he said.

"Ain't it the truth," I agreed.

Wyatt's relationship to Doc and me changed at that moment.

I knew the code the two men shared.

Doc was loyal to Wyatt because of how he'd helped him back at the Flat.

But now, Wyatt owed Doc his life.

That meant that he owed him his unswerving loyalty for as long as he lived.

And, I knew that from that, it followed that Wyatt Earp would never again fuck me for as long as Doc was still alive.

Well, I would miss Wyatt Earp's glorious cock.

And maybe, just maybe, I could reclaim it some day.

But not so long as Doc Holliday lived.

Chapter Ten

DOC'S LAST GAMBLE

In January, 1880, Wyatt Earp got a telegram from John C. Frémont, who was governor of the Arizona Territory.

What it amounted to was that he would appoint Wyatt United States Marshal for the Tombstone Region. What was more, he would appoint any and all of Wyatt's brothers as deputy marshals.

The region was lawless and the sheriff, John Behan, was a crony of the cattle rustlers, stage coach robbers, and other assorted gunslingers who had made Tombstone their area.

The Earp bothers were all in different towns around the West.

Writing and telegraphing each other, they agreed to meet in Tucson and ride down into Tombstone together.

Wyatt asked Doc if he'd like to come along.

.....

Doc talked to me about it.

"Kate, I've decided to go down to Tombstone with Wyatt and his brothers.

"I'm dying, Darling. And I know it. I've never kidded myself about my end. I've been wasting away before your eyes ever since Leadville.

"Eight years ago, I was diagnosed with consumption and given six months to live.

"For the last eight years Death has been my constant companion.

"I've gotten to know him so well, I have no fear of him whatsoever.

"My lungs are finally shot all to Hell. I know, and I know you know, I can't hang in there for more than six months now.

"As a gambler, I've beaten the odds all to Hell.

"So I plan to go to Tombstone. And I'll ride with Wyatt. In that hellhole of a town the odds are stacked against us.

"Wyatt, his five brothers, and I will be standing up against hundreds of the meanest sons of bitches left in the West.

"If I'm lucky, one of the bastards will outdraw me and I'll die with my boots on. I've never let any motherfucker get the draw on me. And I won't out there. But if someone manages to do so, it will be an appropriate end to a shootist like me.

"But if I survive Tombstone, I'll get on my horse and ride out into that endless desert, and ride, and ride, until dehydration and starvation make me food for the vultures.

"So, when I ride out of Dodge, it's goodbye, Kate. We've had lots of good times, and some great fights.

"But where I'm going, you can't follow."

I thought that was a mighty pretty speech.

And I knew I wasn't going to follow Doc west to watch him die.

So I didn't say a word.

Instead, we fucked up a mighty storm.

. . . . .

Before he headed west, Wyatt came to see me, of course.

And I thought he made a pretty good speech.

What do you think?

He said:

"Well, Kate. Doc and me are heading out tomorrow to meet my brothers in Tucson.

"Then we'll all get ourselves down to Tombstone to straighten things out down there for the governor.

"I suspect we'll be successful. But you never know.

"Personally, if I survive, I'll be heading from there for California. Not as a lawman. Tombstone's my last stand doing that.

"I hear there's good business in San Diego for a saloon keeper. And that's what I intend to be.

"If you ever think of looking me up, I'll be in the Stingaree Quarter there in San Diego.

"That is, if I survive Tombstone.

"So long."

Now what the Hell was the man with the golden cock telling me?

Damned if I know.

Do you?

.....

I waved Doc and Wyatt off at the railroad station. No tears.

.....

That was a year ago.

And here I am in San Diego. In the Stingaree Quarter as they call it.

I haven't received any letters of any kind from Doc or Wyatt. I didn't expect to.

Six months ago in a copy of the San Diego Union, there was a big story with the dateline of Tombstone, Arizona.

It said there was a big shootout there at the O.K. Corral between the Earp brothers and the Clanton gang.

All the casualties reported were on the Clanton side.

It said Doc Holliday was with the Earps. And that he survived.

From what I can gather, the Earps are scheduled to leave Tombstone any day now.

.....

There've been several rumors around about Doc.

Some say they've heard he went up to a tuberculosis sanitarium in Colorado to die.

I don't hold any truck with that. Doc would never go anyplace to die in a hospital bed.

One gent told me he'd heard Doc went back to Georgia to die in the arms of a sweetheart he'd left back there when he headed west.

Bullshit! I never heard a word from him about some southern belle he'd left behind.

And if he had gone back there, dying in her arms was not like anything Doc would do.

No one has rumored anything about what I know must have become of him.

. . . . .

Doc Holliday was a man who was always true to his word.

Out somewhere in the Great Sonora Desert, there are some bones picked clean by the vultures.

Mister Death has met Doc Holliday on Doc's terms. I am positive in my heart that Doc died with his boots on.

PART TWO

CALAMITY JANE

SHAGS WILD BILL HICKOK

Chapter One

NICE TO MEET YOU

My legal name is Martha Jane Cannary Hickok. And if you call me that I'll knock you flat on your fucking ass.

Everyone out here calls me Calamity Jane. That's because years back I was riding my horse out by Goose Creek in Wyoming. Right before my eyes I saw a band of Injuns fighting our soldier boys and a captain named Egan got an arrow shot into his leg. I lifted the captain onto my horse, got his ass outta there, and set him down back at his camp.

I came by to see him after the sawbones got the God damned arrow outta him. From then on, I took care of his wound until it healed. The captain looked up at me from his hospital tent cot and said, "I name you Calamity Jane, the heroine of the plains."

After that, whenever I was anywhere near a calamity, I dove right in and helped straighten things out.

So now that you know how to call me by the name I go by, I'll let you buy me a drink. Rye if they've got it in this here saloon.

.....

Oh, about the Hickok part of my name. Wild Bill and I were traveling together on our way to Abilene. He got a flesh wound from a band of desperados that swooped down on us. Between Bill and me, we finished off the bastards with our rifles and six-shooters. But Bill needed some nursing help. And if I do say so myself, I'm the best God damned fucking nurse west of the Kansas border.

While I tended him, we fell in love. As luck would have it, a preacher, Reverend W.F. Warren, hitched us up nice and legal.

Right away, Wild Bill denied we were married. And I understood why and agreed with him. Bill was a great pussy hound. He claimed he'd fucked as many women and killed as many men as the number of days he'd been alive since he was sixteen. If word was to've got out he was married to me, gals would've be scared away from him, thinking I'd be after 'em with my trusty six-shooter.

As for me, I love pussy, too. And cocks as well. I don't much care whether I score cocks or pussy. But I try to average one fuck a day of one or the other.

Truth is, I'll fuck just about anything. One time, out in the woods, I was real horny and I let a nine hundred pound, slavering grizzly bear fuck me. That was one damned hot bruin, let me tell you. You don't believe me? Try it some time. You'll like it. If you survive, that is.

Bill lied to everyone that he was married to some circus owner named Agnes Lack Back East. That's so he'd seem off limits matrimony wise to the cunts who wanted to wrap a ring around his finger. But I, and only I, was his legally married wife – and now, of curse, his widow.

And I'll drink to that. Thank you, Pilgrim.

. . . . .

That's one of the ways Bill managed to deal with women. Of course, he didn't know women like I know men. Hardly any females even know how to deal with men like I do. I've lived like a man, dressed like a man, worked like a man, and fucked like a man...and like a woman, too. Gals see me with a group of guys, getting along with them, they tell me they'd like to understand the other sex as well as I do. I've worked right along beside 'em as a mule skinner, a bullwhacker, and a stage coach driver. I've hunted with the hunters, scouted with the scouts, and gone pussy hunting with the pussy hunters. As a result, I've learned what makes every God damned male in the West tick. He's always in one of two states.

Gals ask me, "What are those two states, Jane?" I tell 'em a man's always either thirsty or horny. I'll bet you didn't know that either, did you? I'll let you buy me another shot of rye if I tell you what good it does to know that little gem abut men – paper-collars, pilgrims, dudes, lawmen or desperados.

If that hunk of meat ain't got a hardon, give him a shot of rye.

And that, Pilgrim, is Calamity Jane's recipe for getting along with men.

You can buy me another shot of that fucking rotgut now if you'd like.

.....

You were probably wondering how I ended up here in Deadwood. Well, I guess I wouldn't be here if the citizens in Abilene hadn't got all pissy-pissy. You know Wild Bill was marshal of that God damned burg. There was no law and order when he and Colorado Charlie and me got there. He cleared up the place.

While he was there the pilgrims could hardly get drunk and disorderly without getting one of Bill's slugs in their bellies or get hauled off peaceable to the calaboose. Bill even shot one of his own cops.

That was by mistake, of course. He mistook that deputy for someone else. Hell, anyone can make a mistake or two, can't he?

Well, the powers in town got good and sick of law and order and turned against Bill. After all he'd done for the cocksuckers you'd think they would've been appreciative, wouldn't you?

The God damned saloonkeepers and whoremasters got up a petition with a list of "undesirables" whose likes were "not to be tolerated in Abilene." Guess who the three "undesirables" were? Number one was Wild Bill Hickok. Number two was Colorado Charlie Utter. And number three, fuck their rotten souls to Hell, was Calamity Jane Cannary. The motherfuckers didn't even know my name was Calamity Jane Hickok. But I guess I can't blame 'em for that. Bill insisted, after all, that we keep a lid on that bit of intelligence.

The bad part, though, was this. At the head of the fucking petition were the names of the same sons of bitches who'd begged Bill to be marshal there in the first place.

Bill, Charlie, and me didn't leave that asshole of a town because we were run out. No, siree. We left in disgust. Fuck those bastards. We wouldn't stay in Abilene if they'd of begged us on bended knee. They can kiss their own fucking asses. We were out of there.

We went to Cheyenne. But we weren't too well received there either. Bill found it hard to score pussy in Cheyenne and Charlie and I weren't able to get our daily quota of cock. It just wasn't a friendly town. And besides, the card players were shy of high stakes. At least when Bill was at the tables.

Bill said to Charlie and me one day, "I'm sick of this cheapskate, piss-poor excuse of a town. They've hit gold in the Black Hills, up in Dakota Territory. Miners have gold and they can't wait to gamble it away. What do you two say to going up there?"

Colorado Charlie's a Mountainman. But he's also one hell of a horse driver and can manage a wagon train better than anyone I ever knew. Except me, of course. He'd managed a stage coach line back in Colorado, and ran provision lines to mining camps up there. With the Black Hills being newly opened up he saw the possibility of running a coach line or provision wagons, or both, from Cheyenne or Fort Laramie to Deadwood. So he was all for going there and checking it out. And besides, I know he was thinking there'd be more fresh asses to fuck and cocks to suck in the Black Hills than he was likely to find sticking around in Cheyenne.

And, of course, wherever Wild Bill wanted to go, that's where I wanted to go. That's the one way I was always faithful to my husband.

So Charlie rustled up a couple of wagons, and some mules, and we left Cheyenne for Deadwood. And that's how I got here.

But I didn't make it here as fast as Wild Bill and Colorado Charlie. I'll tell you about that. But, God damn! I've got to take a chaw of 'baccy first. It's hard for me to talk this long without gnawing on a plug. Know what I mean?

Thinking of 'baccy, it's a funny thing about me and Bill and Charlie. We each had a different hankering when it came to 'baccy.

Ptui! Hit that God damned spittoon right in the hole. I just don't miss very fucking often.

Anyway, about us three and 'baccy.

Chewing's the only kind of 'baccy for a bullwhacker or a mule skinner. I've been both so I take mine smokeless. Now Bill, he smoked stogies. A lot of that was for looks. You know about his vanity and the way he was always living up to his image. He liked to dress up real nice and he was real particular about how his hair and nails looked. He figured a stogie went real well with that hat he wore, too.

I don't much give a shit for how I look most of the time. So a wad of chaw in my cheek don't bother my looks one way or t'other.

Charlie smokes pipes. Clay pipes. He's got store-bought teeth you know. He needed to keep his gums in good shape and said there's no better way to keep your gums hard than smoking clay pipes.

Now, about Colorado Charlie. He's queer as fool's gold. He said those gums of his made him a very popular cock sucker. I can see his point. But I'm not about to knock out my teeth and start smoking clay pipes to improve my prospects as a cock sucker. I do just great the way I am, teeth and all. You could have asked Wild Bill, since he got more head from me than I ever gave anyone else.

But you're not here to listen to me run my fucking yap about 'baccy. I was going to tell you about how me and Bill and Charlie hauled ass out of Cheyenne and headed for the Black Hills.

But, I'll tell you what. After I've had a good chaw, I get to hankering for a little shot of rye. What do you think, Pilgrim?

Ptui! Thank you kindly.

. . . . .

We headed north with two wagons. Charlie drove one and I drove the other. Bill rode Black Nell. I don't recall if she was Black Nell III or Black Nell IV. Makes no difference nohow. Bill did all the scouting ahead. He'd talked to every Injun scout in Cheyenne before we left and he figured we'd be clear of Sioux along our way. No roving bands had been seen recently. The three of us knew we could take care of ourselves if we only ran across one or two Injuns out hunting game instead of scalps.

In the evenings when we set up a campfire, we'd sit around after I'd rustled up some grub for us. Bill would practice with his deck of cards.

Wild Bill was a card sharp. That's how he supported himself and me when he wasn't getting paid as a lawman. Poker was his game. He cheated, of course. But he made sure never ever to win real big. If one of the men at the table was losing a lot, Bill would manipulate the cards so the chump could win back enough to leave the table just a little broke, not busted. Know what I mean?

But naturally there were times when he couldn't really rescue the man if he was too shitty a card player.

So Bill would win some and occasionally lose some. He knew big winners can't get people to play with 'em. And, besides, big winners get ambushed by big losers when they get caught off guard.

So on the way to Deadwood, the three of us would sit around the fire at night. Bill would shuffle his deck. I'd say something like "seven of diamonds." Bill would deal out that fucking seven most of the time. Charlie would say, like, "Jack of spades." Damned if that wasn't the next card Bill dealt off the top of the deck. Most of the time.

My job, and Charlie's too, was to spot him doing it. Once in a while I'd catch Bill peeking at a bottom card or flipping one from his sleeve. I'd yell "Fuck!" when I spotted it and Bill would work at doing it again and again until neither Charlie or me could see the slight of hand.

Of course, if anyone accused him to his face of cheating at the table, Wild Bill just shot the guy.

It was Bill's reflexes that made him so good at manipulating the cards. Being the fastest draw in the West kept him alive. Being the slyest card mechanic in the West kept him flush.

When we put out the fire at night and crawled back in the wagons, Bill and me fucked in the wagon and Charlie bedded down in the other one. Bill's fucking was nothing out of the ordinary. He did the standard tit sucking and pussyhandling. Then, we usually ended up doing the missionary position or sometimes the doggie. I'd suck his cock once in a while but Bill never ate my twat. And that was pretty much our love life.

We could've had a problem with Charlie. He had the hots all the time for Wild Bill. And, of course, Bill would have none of that. He knew about Charlie and how he loved to suck cock and assfuck and get assfucked. But Charlie's sexual tastes didn't bother Bill one fucking bit. Wild Bill was real open minded 'bout what didn't really concern him. But he made it real clear to Charlie, or to anyone else for that matter, that he only swung one way himself.

When Charlie was all snuggled down in his wagon he could hear Bill and me fucking away. Our wagons were kept side by side and sounds carry out there on the prairie.

So, to keep Charlie from getting all grumpy and hard to get along with, I'd go over to his wagon after Bill and me were through and let that Colorado man fuck me in the ass. He'd pretend I was a boy. And taking it in the asshole never bothered me none and it made Charlie feel good. So what the Hell, eh?

.....

Well, Sir, we'd set off from Cheyenne on June 27, 1876. I'm not real big on keeping track of calendar dates. Out here it's more important to pay attention to what the skies and the earth and the grasses are telling you about the day rather than what some fucking calendar is saying. But Bill and Charlie had talked so much about leaving on June 27 that the date has kinda stuck in my head. And the other date I know for sure is July tenth. That's the date Wild Bill and Colorado Charlie pulled into Deadwood. That's a date that's mentioned a lot out here. It was a big date for Deadwood because Wild Bill Hickok's arrival in any town in the West is a red letter day for the pilgrims.

.....

I know the first thing Bill and Charlie did when they got to Deadwood, they set up two tents and then headed for the bathhouse. Just the two of 'em, because I wasn't there myself. I got sidetracked on the way from Cheyenne to Deadwood. I want to tell you about the detour I made.

I think it was just after July fourth. I'm not real sure 'cause we weren't keeping track of any kinda calendar and so didn't even shoot off our guns for the Fourth of July on account of we didn't fucking even know it *was* the Fourth. Anyway, whether it was July fourth or fifth or sixth, what the fuck does it matter?

I can tell you where it happened, though. We'd just gotten past a little settlement called Four Corners where the main trail is crossed by an old Injun hunting path. A scraggly bunch of settlers had built some sod houses there that didn't amount to much. We stopped by to shoot the shit with 'em some and learned that no Injuns had bothered 'em. That was good news for travelers like us.

A day's ride beyond Four Corners we'd set up our overnight camp. The next morning we were stretching and yawning by the breakfast campfire when a real handsome road agent wearing a mask comes barging into our camp. We all had spotted him from a distance and wondered who the Hell would be out on the plains at that time in the morning and what the fuck he'd be up to.

When the highwayman hove into our camp Bill ordered him off his horse and told him to drop his pistol and unmask. The dude dismounted all right, but didn't take off his mask. And he had his six-shooter in his hand when he hit the ground.

From the moment I saw him coming, fifteen minutes before he got to our camp, I'd kept my bullwhip in my hand. With my blacksnake I can flick a fly off the ear of an ox at twenty feet. Shit, any bullwhacker can do that. It's a requirement for the job. So as soon as the road agent got off his horse and still had his gun in hand, I flicked that fucking pistol right outta his hand with the blacksnake.

He jumped up and down, doing a kinda little dance. He shook his hand and blew on it, and yipped like some of those fool little dogs some of the whores bring out West with 'em.

"Ow, that smarts," he complained. "What did you have to go and do *that* for? My gun wasn't even loaded."

I told him, "You damned fool. If I hadn't disarmed you, Wild Bill would've plugged you."

He looked real careful at the three of us. "Wild Bill Hickok?" he gasped, while continuing to shake his hand as if he could get the sting out of it that way. "Golly, Hi, Wild Bill."

"That's Mister Hickok to you, Sonny," Bill said. He hated it when a stranger didn't address him proper like. He was a great one for people showing respect.

"Oh, yeah," the stranger said. "Sorry, Mister Hickok. No disrespect meant. And I didn't mean no harm. I'm Deadwood Dick, myself. A famous and well-feared road agent in these here parts. I'm plumb glad to meet you all. All three of you, that is. And I'm glad, too, that you didn't shoot me. Like I said, that pistol of mine laying there on the ground, it ain't loaded. I never carry a loaded gun. I wouldn't want to hurt no one."

Well, I wanna tell you something. I fell like a ton of buffalo shit for that road agent who went around without any bullets in his repeater. Mask or no mask, he was a mighty pretty hunk of young man. Not as handsome as Wild Bill. I never saw a man in all my life as good looking as Bill. But this boy was still a real piece of eye candy, I'll tell you.

"How do you like him, Calam?" Bill asked me.

"I'd like to give him a good fucking," I said.

I looked over at Charlie and from his expression I could see that he would've like to do the same thing.

Bill spoke to the mild-mannered highwayman.

"Tell you what I'll do, Deadwood Dick. This little lady here, she's all tuckered out from having to drive this God damned wagon all the way here from Cheyenne. She needs a rest. So, if you'll take her somewhere on that horse of yours off to your hideout where she can rest up a few days, then deliver her to Deadwood in five days or so from now, I know she'll be much obliged. And so will my pard here and me. 'Cause that'll save us from having to dig a grave over yonder to bury you in . What do you think?"

Deadwood Dick thought it was a good idea for Wild Bill not to shoot him dead and have to bury him. So he picked up his unloaded gun off the ground and got back up on his horse. Bill and Charlie hoisted me up so I could ride pillion. Deadwood Dick and me waved goodbye to Bill and Charlie, and away we rode off East to Dick's hideaway up in the Black Hills, Dakota Territory.

.....

Around noon we came to a settlement called Whoopville. It wasn't much more of a town than Four Corners but it did have a small shanty with a saloon sign posted outside.

When we hauled up in front of the Bailey Saloon and got off the horse, a dozen or so people came out onto the road to greet Deadwood Dick. His masked appearance didn't seem to alarm 'em at all.

I asked him 'bout that.

"You see, Ma'am," he drawled. "What I do is steal from the rich and give to the poor. If it warn't for me, these folks would've starved 'cause it's a hard-scrabble life out here. So I always get a nice warm reception when I stop by or even when I'm just passing through."

I'd heard stories 'bout road agents who robbed from the rich to give to the poor. But I always thought it was a hundred percent horseshit.

Deadwood Dick was that kind of crook according to him. Which in my book made him fucking nuts. Which didn't make him any the less eye candy. You have to be pretty weird out here to make me shun you. I wasn't going to make up my mind about him until I had taken full measure of his peter.

We went into the little shack of a saloon. A long, thin drink of water in an apron greeted us.

"Deadwood Dick," he enthused. "Welcome to Whoopville."

"Howdy, Ben," Dick said. "Thank you. I'd like you to meet…uh…uh…"

It hadn't occurred to him before to ask who I was.

I couldn't let him stammer and suffer like such a horse's ass so I walked right up to the host or barkeep or whatever the fuck the cocksucker was.

"Calamity Jane Cannary," I said as I grabbed his hand and shook it.

"I should of knowed," Ben said. "You're the most famous lady in all the West. What can I get you?"

"You got any rye whiskey?" I asked.

"Sure, sure. Sit down. I'll be right over with a bottle. Will rye do for you, Deadwood Dick?"

"Rye's fine," Dick answered.

We pulled a couple of rickety chairs up to a wobbly plank table. My ass was sore from riding pillion so far, but the chair felt good anyway.

"Golly," Dick said. "You're Calamity Jane. Dang! I didn't know who you were. Pleased to meet you, Ma'am."

"Cut the ma'am shit, Good Looking," I told him. "My friends call me Calam. And I intend for you and me to be real good friends. Do you fuck?"

I've never been backward about laying it on the line. There are folks who hem and haw and waste a lot of time beating around the bush. If there's a stud or a studette makes my twat quiver, I get to the point right away and then we both know where we're heading.

"Now that you mention it, Calm," he answered. "I'm very partial to poontang. Most of it I get here is Squaw. And it's not bad, but tends to be kinda unimaginative, if you know what I mean."

Nut case or not, and even if he really does rob to give the loot away, I knew this pilgrim was going to be a Hell of a fuck. Wild Bill had done me a big favor sending me off with the masked wonder.

Ben brought over a bottle and two jelly glasses. The bottle didn't have a label, but out this way that's not too unusual.

"We've got some buffalo stew and pan bread on the menu," Ben told us.

I could see that whiskey, buffalo stew, and pan bread was all there was in the joint. So that's what we ordered.

I took a snort of the whiskey. Now I've had bad whiskey afore. Stuff that'll take the hair right off your bean. But the stuff in that bottle looked and smelled like mule piss. And it tasted even worse. But I drank it without a whimper and so did my date.

"So you're Calamity Jane and the guy who nearly plugged me is Wild Bill Hickok," Dick said when his eyes cleared up after taking a gulp of the rotgut. "Who was the other guy? Mister Hickok's pard?"

"Colorado Charlie Utter," I told him.

"Golly. The best mountain man in the West. And I didn't even shake his hand."

"Your hand was in no shape to shake Charlie's," I told him. "The sting of my blacksnake is usually enough to put whatever it hits out of commission for a spell."

I'd decided Deadwood Dick was going to be my sweetie. It's good to have a husband, a sweetie, and as many occasional lays as you can fit in around 'em.

My sweetie looked kinda embarrassed about my mentioning how I'd disarmed him, so I changed the subject.

"How far is it to this here hideout you're taking me to?" I asked.

Ben came along with a couple of tin plates full of about the mangiest looking stew I ever saw. Or smelled. He looked real pleased with what he was offering us.

I hoped to Hell my boyfriend had better fixings than this up to his place. If not, I'd have to go out and hunt us some decent game and gather some herbs and rustle us up some decent grub. And if he didn't have better whiskey than this piss we were drinking, he'd get a quick fuck and suck and I'd cut my vacation with him real short.

Dick got around to answering my spoken question and the one he musta read from my mind.

"My hideaway's 'bout another three hour ride into the hills. It's actually in a cave, but it's a real nice cave. And I've robbed enough provision trains to get plenty of good rye whiskey in from the States and from Canady. And food? Hams and tinned meat and corn and taters and some cans of stuff I don't even know what they are but they're good eating."

I knew we were going to have ourselves a time when we got to his God damned cave.

. . . . .

That masked doll was right about the three hour ride up into the Black Hills. From a distance, you'd think those hills were a kind of pale purple color. As your horse begins to climb, the deep green pine trees take over so the God damned hills get to looking darker and darker. It's Sioux country and the U.S. Government wants us White folk to keep the fuck out. Hah! With all that gold in those creeks? Don't make me laugh.

We was heading towards a peak. Deadwood Dick didn't know if it had a name. I found out later someone named it Harney Peak. I don't think no Redskin gave it a name like that.

We didn't actually get to that fucker, but we were pretty high up in the hills anyway.

We came to a meadow and Dick told me we'd arrived. I was off the horse faster than he was and I started right off rubbing my ass to get some blood flowing through the tingles. My sweetie tethered the horse to a pine tree and led me to the edge of the meadow. There was a knoll there that was heavily covered with chaparral.

"This is it, Calam," the gorgeous fucker said with a smile.

"This is *what* Sweet Stuff?" I asked.

"My hideaway...your hideaway," he laughed.

He opened a kinda gate that was so covered with the dense growth you'd never know it was there. I'm telling you, Pardner, no one, not even an Injun or Colorado Charlie could ever have known there was an entrance to a cave hidden there. But there was, and is.

Deadwood Dick and I went in and he closed the fucking gate. We were in a limestone cavern, with a hole above us you could see the sky through. That hole must be a least twenty-five feet up on the top of the knoll. It let light in and smoke out.

Dick had the place fixed up real comfortable. The main cavern is about seven or eight hundred square feet in size. He had it furnished with real nice stuff he'd lifted from the supply wagons down on the plains. There's a passageway off to one corner that leads down into a deeper cavern. Holding a lantern, he led me down there. I'll be a cocksucker if it wasn't cool as could be in that lower cavern. And it was loaded with enough meat and vegetables to take care of a pack of hungry bullwhackers. Well, there *was* enough food there, which I guess, proves I *am* a cocksucker. I was reserving that treat for my newfound boyfriend.

Heading on our way back into the main cavern I could see that Deadwood Dick was thinking the same thing I was, and it wasn't food. He was wearing a hardon that showed he had what I wanted.

But, being a gentlemanly kind of robber, he didn't hustle me right over to the enormous bed in the corner. Instead, from over on a shelf, he pulled down a bottle of Old Potrero rye whiskey. Jesus!

When I get to Heaven and the Good Lord asks me how I want to be rewarded for the virtuous life I've led, I'm going to tell the Big Guy to lay me down on a bed under a limitless barrel of Old Potrero and let me guzzle for Eternity.

Dick opened the bottle, poured us each a slug of that stuff, and the party was off to a great start.

And thinking of that bottle just kinda gives me a thirst. How 'bout you? Can I buy you a drink? Oh, well. If you insist, I don't mind if I do. Thankee.

. . . . .

Now where was I? Oh, yes, about how Deadwood Dick and me got it on.

As my friend Al Swearengen always says, "A fuck is *always* good. But some's better than others."

I've already told you that my husband, Wild Bill, is only a fair fuck. Not to put him down. I loved it when we screwed. You know yourself how handsome he was and that counts for a lot. But once he got his rocks off, it was like you weren't there any more. Know what I mean? He was tall and thin and that long thin prick of his fitted him just fine. And I loved him more than I've ever loved any man before or since. Or any woman either, for that matter.

But as a lover, Deadwood Dick was really tops. God, how that man could fuck. His prick ain't all that long. It's long enough to do a lady good, but not like Bill's. Dick's is thick and can fill a hole so you feel every blood vessel and every ridge along it right up and down the whole cunt channel. Now *that's* something a girl like me, who's been fucked by a nine hundred pound grizzly bear with slavering jaws, can really appreciate. That bear was the best lover I ever had. But, for human companions, I've gotta put Deadwood Dick way up on the list.

There's one other little thing that makes him special – he fucks with his mask on. He was the only man I've fucked in the light whose whole face I'd never seen. Of course, there've a few men I did in the dark, but that's another story you might wanna hear sometime.

Deadwood Dick doesn't just fuck you and forget you like some people I could name. He may not have any bullets for his six-shooter. But he has loads of refills in his balls. I've never known anyone with that stamina. Not even Bosco.

"Who's Bosco?" you ask.

I don't ordinarily let that information out. Bosco is the name I gave to the grizzly. Kinda fits, don't it?

But to get back to Dick. We fucked and sucked and licked and handled and went up one side of each other and down the other. It's like a song that Lilly Langtree or some other of them warbling dames sing over at the Gem. "I fucked him standing and I fucked him lying. And if he'd had wings I'd of fucked him flying."

We did each other all night. We stopped for a breakfast of flapjacks, bacon, and coffee. Then we went at it again 'til the middle of the afternoon.

We took a rest, and then tumbled and sported 'til dinnertime.

.....

That went on day after day after day. But Dick had pretty much agreed to get me to Deadwood after my "rest" of five days or so.

After four days of getting pleasured by my sweetie, my twat was so red and swollen that I knew it would about kill me to ride pillion on into Deadwood if we tumbled in that bed one more time. And Dick's poor peter was becoming a bloody mess. So it was time to get back on the road. I didn't think either of us was up to taking any more pleasure for a spell.

Dick, being a masked desperado, couldn't just ride into Deadwood with me behind him, drop me off, and ride calmly away. There was a price on his head, and he wasn't anxious for anyone to get the reward. That would end up with him getting a suspended sentence with a rope around his own neck.

So we rode back the way we came.

When we got to Whoopville, Dick asked me if I wanted to stop at the saloon. I'd brought along a bottle of Dick's Old Potrero with us, and wasn't real interested in swilling down the mule piss that passes for rye at Ben Bailey's tavern. And we'd brought along some buffalo jerky. I had a couple of plugs of 'baccy with me. Deadwood Dick smoked cigareets and had brought a couple of packs along. So we just nodded howdy to the folks in Whoopville and went on to Four Corners.

On the way there we finished off the Old Potrero and the jerky. And we enjoyed our 'baccy right along with our vittles and drink.

.....

When we got almost to Four Corners, we ran into a traveling man hauling a cartload of cats up the trail. Dick pulled his gun on him.

"I'm Deadwood Dick, the scourge of the West," he announced.

"All I've got is these God damned cats," the traveling man answered. back. "You want a cat? Put that motherfucking gun away and help yourself."

Dick told the man he'd kidnapped me, had been paid his ransom, and had to return me back to Deadwood.

"I'm on my way to Deadwood with these God damned cats," the man said. "I'd be more than happy to have the little lady's company."

So it was arranged. I told the cat man I was a Hell of a wagoneer and would love to spell him off along the way. He looked doubtful about my abilities along that line. I proved to him later that I was Hell on wheels with horses and wagons.

I got into the wagon seat, Deadwood Dick gave a bloodcurdling cry, and off he rode back to his hideout. I knew I'd miss him. But I needed time for my pussy to heal before I wanted to lay eyes on him again.

.....

We headed off for Deadwood with that wagonload of cats.

"What's your name, Gal? the wagoneer asked me.

"Calamity Jane Cannary," I told him. "My friends call me Calam."

"Well I'll be a God damned cockeyed cocksucker," he replied. "I've driven this fucking wagon all over the shit-eating West. San Fran, Yuma, Abilene...you name it,. Every city, town, settlement or camp I've been to, people're blabbing this, that and t'other thing about Calamity Jane. A plague hits, Calamity Jane's nursing the sick. A gal gets abused, it's always Calamity Jane to the rescue. A man's going off his fucking noodle from lack of nookie, it's Calamity Jane to relieve him of his misery.

I'm right pleased to meet you Miss Calm. Me, I'm Phatty Thompson, the most traveled wagoneer in the West."

We shook hands.

"Glad to meet you, too, Phatty," I said. And I meant it.

He wasn't much to look at. He was short, squat, and his beard was about as scraggly as they get. I found out his first name really was Phatty. He musta been as plump a little baby as he was as a geezer to land him a name like that. But I thought spelling the name with a "Ph" instead of an "F" showed pretty good taste on the part of Mister and Missus Thompson.

"How many cats have you got in those crates back there?" I asked him.

"Eighty-two," he said and slapped his thigh. He seemed real proud. I guessed that was some kinda record for cats in wagons or something like that.

I asked him why he was hauling eighty-two fucking cats to Deadwood.

"I thought you'd ask that, Calam. Everyone says you got the best brain of any gal in the West. Always inquiring and finding out what's going on. So, a gal like you, she's shit-sure to wanna know why a fucking old geezer like me is hauling eighty-two cocksucking cats from Cheyenne to Deadwood. I'll tell you why."

Before he was prepared to go into his spiel, he reached into a poke and drew out a wad of 'baccy.

"Care for a God damned chaw, Calam?" he asked.

I bit a chew off the wad and handed it back to him. He took a chaw himself and dropped the wad back into the poke.

"You're a real gentleman, Phatty," I said. "Man who offers a lady a chaw before he takes one himself is real fucking chivalrous. Thank you."

"My momma taught me how to fucking treat a lady," he claimed. "Just because I gave you a chaw don't mean I think you owe me a fucking right away. No siree. I was raised better than that."

With the way my twat was still red and raw from my continuous days of doing Deadwood Dick and being done by him, I knew Phatty wasn't gonna get to fuck me for a chaw of 'baccy anyway. But I didn't bother to tell him so at the time.

Having gotten through the formality of sharing a wad and a little spitting match that we didn't mention to each other but that I won, he told me 'bout why we were hauling that caterwauling cargo on the wagon.

"You ever hear of Madame Moustache?" he asked.

As a matter of fact I had heard her name mentioned in some of the places I'd visited, but I really didn't know too much about her.

"I'm familiar with the name," I told him. "But I'd like to hear about her firsthand from you. French gal, ain't she? Worked the mining camps out in Californy? Deals blackjack or something?"

"That's the gal," Phatty assured me. "She used to clean the boys out dealing twenty-one. She got run outta San Fran, then outta Calaveras, nearly got lynched up at Hangtown outside Sacramenty.

"To save her neck, she headed out this way and shifted to operating a faro bank.

"She don't cheat at faro very much and makes up for the slower action at the table by plying her other two trades."

"Which are?" I prompted.

"Cock sucking and spiritualizing."

I certainly knew what cock sucking was, being what people call an "adept" at the practice myself. But spiritualizing was something I didn't know about.

"What the fuck is 'spiritualizing'?" I asked him.

"You know," he said. "She talks to the God damned spirits."

"Dead fuckers?" I asked.

"You got it. Anyone wants to know what's going to happen to 'em in the future, Madame Moustache asks the fucking ghosts and they tell her."

"Did you ever ask her about the future?" I questioned him.

"Fuck, no," he spit. "I got enough on my hands with the present. I'll let the fucking future take care of itself. What I wanted from the Madame was to get my knob polished. And, by God, I wasn't disappointed in that."

I spit out a spurt of 'baccy juice and waited for Phatty to expand however he wanted. He liked to talk so all it took was some patience on my part to find out what the famous Madame Moustache had to do with a God damned wagonload of squalling, fucking, fighting cats.

"Now I've had my cock sucked in more cities, towns, encampments and one-horse towns than anyone West of the Mississip' except maybe Wild Bill Hickok," Phatty bragged.

Whoa! Phatty was beginning to tread on personal ground here.

Of course, he didn't know he was mentioning my husband. But I knew Wild Bill was more addicted to missionary position fucking than getting his knob polished. Not that he didn't relish a little tune on his skin flute from time to time. But he would not be pleased to hear someone suggesting that he was in competition with a wagoneer named Phatty Thompson for the number of times he got that long, thin peter of his played on by female lips. But I wasn't about to correct Phatty and cut his story short.

He spit a pretty good one off to the side of the wagon and continued.

Ptui! Hell, a lady can develop a thirst rattling on like this, you know.

. . . . .

"Madame Moustache came to Deadwood last year. She's there now, operating a faro bank at Jim Persate's Wide West Saloon. It's at Main and Gold Streets if you'd like to check it out sometime. It's the most honest game in Deadwood right now. Which ain't saying much, I'll admit," Phatty said.

"When I'm in Deadwood I hang out at the Wide West and I don't do too bad playing faro there. But I spend all my winnings and a lot more in Madame Moustache's upstairs room where she gives me her special.

"What she does is something no other cock sucker can do. If you ever meet her, though, don't call her a cock sucker. She gets kinda riled up at the term. She says that over there in Paris, France they call her an 'arteest.' That's what you've got to call her if you want her to give your cock a number one suck."

I good-naturedly told Phatty she couldn't do that.

"Do what?" he asked.

"Give my cock a number one suck," I said.

"Why the fuck not?" he asked.

"'Cause I ain't got one," I replied and spit out a gob.

I thought he'd laugh his ass off.

"You got me there, Gal," he said, matching my 'baccy shot for distance. "But you might want to try the Madame if you like your cunt licked. I'll bet she'd do you real fine."

I tucked that idea away for future reference. I would definitely pay the lady a visit when I got to Deadwood. But I still didn't know what she did different from any other cock sucker.

Phatty told me.

"What this here French lady does, she takes your cock and your balls all together in her yap."

He looked at me slyly.

"I mean mine, not yours, of course. It's just a manner of speaking."

I assured him I understood.

"And with the rod and the fambly jewels all inside her mouth she somehow sucks up on your peter and gives a separate suck on your balls all at the same time. And with her moustache dusting the slobber off your dick, you get little shudders running up and down your spine. God damn if that ain't 'bout the grandest cock sucking in the world. It makes your eyes bug right outta your head. That gal gets my trade every time, I'll be a son of a bitch if she don't."

I've had enough dongs in my mouth to know that trick Phatty described could only be done by someone with a mighty big cavern of a mouth or to a man with a mighty small cock and tiny balls. Most guys I've done who were little round butterballs like Phatty were tiny in their equipment. My bet was that Madame Moustache couldn't do that trick with most of the pilgrims she worked. Which meant she probably fitted her technique to the length and thickness of the shaft and the size of the nuts. I'd have to agree that if that was the case, she certainly was an "arteest." It would definitely be worth my while to see what she could do with a snatch.

"Last time the Madame was working on my prick," Phatty continued, "When she'd sucked me dry as the God damned Mojave, I asked her how she like being in Deadwood.

"She says to me in that sexy French accent, 'Deadwood is the shits. And the worst thing about it is, I do not have my Fifi here with me.'

"I asked her what the fuck a 'Fifi' is. And what do you think she told me?"

I got it in a flash and told him what I thought.

"I'll bet the fambly farm that Fifi was some God damned cat she'd had."

"Yep," Phatty agreed. "When she'd got run outta Calaveras, she had to hightail it out of there so fast she had to leave her fucking cat behind. And she hadn't been anywhere since then where she could get a replacement.

"So I got me an idea. I sez to her, 'How much would you be willing to pay for a kitty?'

"She told me she'd pay ten bucks for just any old cat. But for Maltese like Fifi she'd pay twenty-five.

"'Whoa!' I sez to myself. 'There just might be something here where a feller can get more fucking gold from kittycats than he can panning in that freezing Whitewood Creek.' So I made the rounds of the dancehalls and whorehouses. Damn near every one of the cunts said she'd like a kittycat.

"What's more, the God damned town's over-run with rats and mice. You think you can find one fucking mousetrap at Bullock and Star's store? Or at Liebman's? No siree. Every last jack cook in town, including Chinatown, wanted a fucking cat.

"I went and built me those crates you see back there and loaded 'em on this here wagon. I climbed in and pushed off for Cheyenne. I got word out to every urchin in Cheyenne I could reach. Told 'em I'd pay two cents per cat for every one they brought me that was in good condition. I'll be a fly on a horse turd if those boys didn't round up those eighty-two fucking, fighting meowing bunch of felines you hear raising that ruckus behind us. I went to a bunch of butcher shops and restaurants and bought me chicken heads for a penny apiece. That's what you smell back there other than cat farts. When we pull over for the night I throw the chicken heads into the crates. You'll get a kick outta it tonight for sure. It's a real circus seeing those cats go after that chow."

He spit out a squirt and I matched it for distance.

"Yes, indeedy," he chuckled. "I aim to make me a fortune with all that pussy."

So Phatty was hauling pussy to Deadwood. He and I joked about that.

.....

That evening we pulled the wagon over and camped a short jaunt from where the trail crosses the Cheyenne River at Edgemont.

While Phatty started the campfire, I threw chicken heads into the crates for the cats. The scrambling, fighting, caterwauling, and just plain greedy viciousness of the damned cats was enough to turn you off pussycats for the rest of your life. But I figured we had over a thousand dollars worth of cats in those crates and hoped for Phatty's sake they wouldn't all kill each other over raw chicken heads.

Phatty and I sat looking at the fire and he came around to what I knew he was going to come around to.

"You know, Calm," he began. "The whole time I was in Cheyenne rounding up those God damned cats, I didn't get no pussy."

"There's lots of pussy around in Cheyenne, Phatty," I told him. "I'd say more pussy than cats. So you must not've been real horny."

"I was horny, all right," he claimed. "But I was too busy rounding up the fucking cats to get in any fucking."

"I've known a lot of men in my time," I told him. "And you are the first one I ever met who was too busy to get himself a piece of ass when he was hankering for it. I'll mark you down in my book as the exception that proves the rule."

Of course, he was leading up to propositioning me and I did not have any plans to fuck or suck Phatty Thompson. So I didn't let him play on my sympathies.

"You're a hard woman, Calamity Jane," he complained. "I guess it's not easy to sweet talk you into doing a man some good, is it?"

"I've given a few mercy fucks in my time," I told him. "But right now I'm not up to pleasuring you, Phatty. But I'll tell you what I'll do. Somewhere along the trail I'll give you some relief from your ache. I promise you that. But tonight, it's no use you asking."

That pretty much settled that. We both spit a gob of 'baccy juice into the campfire and lit into a batch of beans and bacon he'd heated up. I still had some Old Potrero and by the time we'd each filled ourselves with his musical fruit and my rye whisky neither of us was up to much in the way of fucky-sucky anyways.

Thinking of that Old Potrero. The barkeep here has some pretty fair rye whisky. And telling my story whumps up a powerful thirst...Thank ye, Pilgrim

.....

The next morning, neither Phatty or I felt too good. The God damn cats were complaining like Hell. So I tossed 'em some chicken heads and we lit out for Hill City.

I started to drive, but Phatty got all pissy about being so horny and complaining about how I'd said I'd relieve him of his blueballs and he was still aching.

After we'd passed Hill City I got sick of his fucking bellyaching.

"Okay, Phatty," I said. "Calamity Jane promised you relief. And Calamity Jane always keeps her word. You're feeling real bad down deep in your nuts. And I have more compassion for you than you can think. You take over the reins and I'll show you how big-hearted Calamity Jane really is." The old guy perked up at that. He took them reins outta my hands and I slid back into the wagon with those God damned cats. The smell of cat shit was enough to make you gag by then. But I'd dealt with all kinds of shit as a mule skinner and a bullwhacker and a ranch hand before. Gagging a little bit never hurt no one.

I dug into Phatty's cooking provisions and got out a tin of bacon grease. I hauled that grease back up to the seat and sat myself next to Phatty.

I reached over and undid the old coot's belt. He perked up real good at that.

The trail was real bumpy between Hill City and Spring Creek. It was tough as Hell to get his pants all unbuttoned. But I'd unbuttoned enough men's pants in my time to manage even tougher situations.

Phatty wanted to help but I insisted he keep his hands on the reins.

He kinda stood up, though, a little so I could lower his pants past his ass. I reached into his union suit and out popped his little pecker.

Just as I'd guessed. It was a pathetic little thing. But it was as eager as all Hell.

I knew that my suspicions were correct about how Madame Moustache got the whole shooting-works into her mouth. It had less to do with the size inside her yap than with the puny size of Phatty's peter. Still, though, that trick of hers in squeezing his balls in one direction and his pecker in the other all inside her mouth showed she really was an *arteest*.

I greased up both my hands real good with the bacon grease. With the way the wagon was bumping along on the trail I knew all I had to do was keep a steady grip on Phatty's cock and balls and the trail would do the rest.

When I grabbed his balls, Phatty let out a whoop like to draw a band of Sioux down on our necks. But I knew the coast was clear of Redskins so he could fucking hoot, whoop, or holler to his heart's content.

Next, my other hand engulfed his itsy-bitsy peter. I think my skillful hands, helped along by the jiggling wagon, had to give him every bit as much pleasure as the Madame's yap.

But I was God damned if I was going to let Phatty have all the fun on this ride. So I kept my left hand on his peter and slipped my right hand off his balls and down inside my own pants. While the wagon was jacking Phatty off, with the help of my left hand grip, the bumpity wagon was working me up to a climax with my bacon-greased finger inserted up my snatch.

We were at the first crossing of Spring Creek. Phatty was a-yipping and a-screaming and just having himself a Hell of a time as the wagon was jacking him off. I got concerned that he was losing control of the fucking horses. But my own finger-fuck had my attention just a mite off the situation.

I took my greasy hands off his cock as he came. As his jism came squirting out all over the place, the God damned wagon swerved, tipped, and fell plumb over on its side just as I came like a band of Apaches myself.

The crates came crashing open and we had eighty-two cats escaping while Phatty was swearing and trying to get his pants back on. I got my finger out of my cunt real fast and went directly up to take care of the horses, who, it turned out, were shaken up but not hurt.

There was a passel of miners working their claims along the creek who dropped everything when they saw cats scattering all over the countryside. A few came over to the wagon to see if we needed any help. Others started collecting the cats to bring 'em back to Phatty.

Phatty quickly got the crates back into holding condition again. As the miners came to him with the cats he told each one he could keep one or two of them himself. I wasn't surprised at how many of those tough hombres thanked Phatty and went away petting and cuddling and talking baby-talk to their new pets. What tenderfeet and paper collars from the East don't know is that us roughnecks out here in the West are really as sensitive inside as they are. We just show it a Hell of a lot different.

Phatty didn't try to count how many cats were retrieved after the accident. He just dropped the critters back in their crates. He thanked the miners and we were on our way again.

I thought he might be gruff or surly at having that accident and losing some of his cats. He wasn't.

He gave the reins to me.

"Here, Gal. You drive. I want to just lay down for a spell and relish that hand job you gave me. I didn't get to enjoy my orgy-asm enough, what with that fucking accident. But you sure know how to handle a man's equipment."

"Nothing to it," I told him as I spit out a spurt of 'baccy. "The bumpy wagon done it all by itself."

Phatty chuckled and climbed back in the wagon and laid down. From his chortles and giggles I could tell he was re-living the ride of his life.

. . . . .

We got to Deadwood the next day. The wagonload of cats was what drew everyone's attention. So I managed to not get noticed too much myself from the townfolk. Which suited me just fine.

I shook hands with Phatty and thanked him for the ride. He thanked me for the ride I'd given him. And that was the last I saw of Phatty Thompson except for one more time at a show he put on at the fence outside the Silver Star Saloon about a month later. He'd sold all his cats except for six toms. He trained them tomcats to entertain. I paid two bits just like every other pilgrim to see the performance. Phatty sat his cat sextet on the fence there and got 'em to yodel for the audience by throwing Swiss cheese at 'em.

I wouldn't of believed yodeling cats myself, Pard, if I hadn't seen it with my own eyes and heard it with my own ears. What it takes, you see, is Swiss cheese.

Whether you believe that or not, the story deserves another shot of rye, don't it?

Chapter Two

WELCOME TO DEADWOOD

Finding the campsite Bill and Charlie had set up didn't require the skills of an army scout. The first person I asked gave me all the information I needed.

"Howdy, Pilgrim," I said to a scruffy looking miner who was hurrying down the road to take a gander at the wagonload of cats that had just arrived in town. "Can you tell me where Wild Bill Hickok and Colorado Charlie have set up camp?"

"Hell, Lady," he answered. "Everybody in town knows that. They're the most famous men who've ever come here."

"I'm new in town myself," I told him. "So I guess I'm the only one don't know. How would I go 'bout finding where the fuck those two famous gentlemen have set up camp?"

"Go right down this here road. It's Main Street. About half a mile down there, on the left, you'll see the Wide West Saloon. On t'other side of the street, the right hand side that is, you'll see the Langrishe Theater. Behind the theater, between Main Street and Sherman Street, you'll see Whitewood Creek. Just on t'other side of the creek there's a kind of tent city. Squatters like me. You get to them tents, ask anyone which one houses Wild Bill."

It was a Hell of a lot more information than I needed, but I thanked the miner for it and he moved his ass real fast like to take a look-see at all them God damned fucking cats everybody was talking 'bout.

I sized up what he'd said and I figured I could get to the site in about half the time if I ducked behind the fucking buildings and just followed the God damn creek. If I could track an Injun out on the plains with half the information the miner gave me, I sure as shit could track down my husband knowing he and Charlie had set up camp somewhere near the fucking creek. And I could see the creek off to my right.

Sure enough, after a ten or fifteen minute walk I picked up the smell of Charlie's pipe tobacco.

Good eyesight, good hearing, and a good sense of smell. Them three things'll get you a long ways out here in the West.

Colorado Charlie spotted me moseying along the creek bank 'bout the time I sniffed his 'baccy. We greeted each other with the bear hug of pardners who've been away from each other too long.

He had his store-bought teeth out of his mouth and was gumming that clay pipe for all he was worth. I took a chaw of 'baccy myself to kinda join in the action.

Charlie indicated the tent that was set up behind him.

"This here one's your tent, Calam. At least as far as anyone 'round here's supposed to know. That one there," he said, pointing his pipe towards a near-by tent, "That one's supposed to be me and Bill's."

I spit a glob in that direction to show I understood.

"When we done got here in Deadwood," Charlie continued, "Me and Bill set up the two tents in tent city right away. The first night, we both slept in that tent. But you know me, Calam. I got me such a painful hardon just a-knowing Wild Bill was next to me that I about lost my fucking mind. So since then, I been sleeping there," he pointed to "my" tent. "Now that you're back with us, I'll bed down in Bill's tent while you crash over there in what we're calling your tent.

"That's for appearance sake. Then, when the coast's clear, you and me'll switch places so's you and Bill can fuck the way you like. Then, afore dawn, you and me'll pull the switcheroo again."

It was the same arrangement as before. None of us wanted it known that Bill and me were married or even that we slept together regularly. Like I told you, Bill didn't want nothing to interfere with his pussy hunting and I was always after fresh dick and cunt. The switches Charlie and I made at night kept the field wide open for Bill's and my foraging for nookie.

"How're you doing, Charlie, in getting your ashes hauled?" I asked.

"You won't have to be concerned about having to take it up the bunghole from me on that account no more here in Deadwood," he assured me. "With all these horny miners everywhere around you look, I get me more action than I know what to do with. I ain't even jacked off once in your absence."

"Hallelujah!" I exclaimed, throwing my hands up.

"Thank you, God!" Charlie answered with the same swoop of his hands.

"Where's Bill now?" I asked.

"Over to the Gem Theater. There's a whore there, Clementine by name, he's got a kind of fancy for."

. . . . .

Now, Stranger. I don't know how well you know your way around Deadwood. You got two kind of theaters here in town. Them with and them without.

"With or without what?" you say.

Whores, of course.

The Langrishe Theater over yonder is the kind of showhouse that puts on plays and musicals. There ain't no upstairs room for fucking there.

The Gem Theater is t'other kind. It's really a saloon, gambling den and a whorehouse with a stage. I knew that if Bill was at a theater, it was *that* kind.

You might want to take the joint in yourself while you're in town. A friend of mine, Al Swearengen, owns and runs the joint. Al's a real cultured whoremaster and whenever a big act comes to town, Al gets 'em on his stage. Hell, Salome, Lily Langtree, Banjo Charlie – all of 'em have played the Gem.

When prizefights come to town, old Al even sets up a regulation ring at the Gem and holds sporting events. I'll tell you 'bout that sometime if you'd like.

I wouldn't mind a little shot of hooch right now. How 'bout you,

Stranger?" Well, thank you kindly

. . . . .

Bill and Charlie are both cleanliness freaks and neatness nuts. I knew that the first thing they would've done after pitching our tents was get down to a bathhouse and wash the trail grime off their bodies. Myself, if it wasn't for keeping myself from smelling too bad to catch me a good flying fuck, I could go bathless a long time. But I was planning on paying Wild Bill a surprise visit. So I knew I'd better hie me over to the bathhouse like my two pards had.

When Deadwood Dick "absconded" with me, Bill and Charlie'd hauled my gear on up here to Deadwood. So I had clean clothes all ready for after a bath. And, of course, I got ahold of my own towel.

You don't ever want to use them towels they give you at any bathhouse west of the Mississip'. They're downright unsanitary.

. . . . .

We had two bathhouses in town back then. We got three now. All of 'em within pissing distance of the creek. I guess they're all about the same. You been down to the one by where Wall Street crosses the creek? I'll tell you about it.

I got down there with my clean clothes and my towel. The attendant's name was something like Sikeshmoot, but he said to just call him Dutch. He asked me if I wanted privacy. That would've cost me a quarter. If I was willing to take my bath with anyone who might come in it would only cost me a dime.

I didn't give a fuck who might come in when I was naked. Hell, let 'em take their chances, says me. So I paid Dutch a dime and entered.

There was three tubs up on a stand so the water could drain out onto the sand outside after you pulled the plug. The bathtubs were filthy, of course, like in every bathhouse I've ever been to. No one scrubs 'em out ever.

There was a big wood stove over to one side of the room with five or six big vats of water heating on it. Next to the stove was another bunch of vats of cold water.

While I'm taking off my duds, Dutch calls out to the Celestial who I seen sitting outside when I approached the joint. I wasn't too surprised. The labor of carrying water from the creek to the bathhouse usually falls to the coolies from Chinatown, which is just north-east of where Sherman runs into Main Street.

The Celestial came in and helped Dutch pour hot water from the stove into the tub and then the two of 'em hauled over a vat of cold water and mixed 'em. Dutch didn't pay me no attention when I went up on the stand to check the temperature of the water. The Celestial couldn't hold back his giggles. I guess he hadn't seen many white gals strutting about in the buff. I was glad to give him a good show.

When I got in the tub Dutch gave me a giant bar of lye soap. That there soap gets passed from one bather to another until it's just a sliver.

Dutch sent the Celestial out to haul some more water from the creek to replace what'd been taken from the two vats. You see a Celestial walking from the creek towards a bathhouse with a long pole on his shoulder and a bucket on each end, you know there's probably someone taking a bath inside the building.

When I got out, all of me, hair, bellybutton, cunt, ass, and feet was so clean you could eat a slab of buffalo steak off any part of me. I was ready to go find Wild Bill.

I went back by the tent then to leave off my dirty clothes. Charlie said he'd take them to Ah-Chin's Laundry and Storage in Chinatown later on with his and Bill's dirties.

I followed the stream back past the bathhouse to get to the Gem Theater. The Gem's about a ten minute walk on beyond where I took my bath.

Far enough to work up a thirst. You wouldn't happen to like to join me for a shot yourself, Stranger? Oh, thank you. Don't mind if I do.

. . . . .

I liked the looks of the Gem right away. The stage isn't one of them tiny jobs you see in most of the "theaters" here in Deadwood. It's worthy of the finer arteests who come here to perform. The mahogany bar goes along a whole wall and it's well stocked. And Jimmy Dougherty, the barkeep, is a real gentleman who knows how to treat a lady.

I walked up to the bar and introduced myself.

"Howdy, I'm Calamity Jane and I'd like a shot of your best rye," I announced.

"Welcome, Miss Calamity," the barkeep smiled. "I'm Jimmy Daugherty and I'm real honored to make your acquaintance. I've got some Old Potrero here behind the bar for our more discriminating guests. Will that do for you?"

"I'd be most obliged, Jimmy," I answered.

He poured me two fingers.

"For a distinguished guest like you, Miss, the first one's on the house."

"Thank ye, Jimmy. And I wish you'd call me Calam 'cause that's what all my friends call me. And I intend that you and me be real good friends. Here's to you."

I downed those two fingers of my favorite booze in one gulp.

I took me a chaw of my 'baccy and said, "I'll take another of them, Jimmy."

I laid a dollar on the bar.

"And keep 'em coming until this bill don't cover 'em no more."

I was drinking and a-chawing and practicing my aim on the shiny brass spittoon when a dapper gentleman came ambling down from the upstairs rooms. He looked me up and down. I looked him up and down. It was clear that we both liked what we saw. He smiled a big broad smile and extended his hand.

"I'll be God damned!" he fairly shouted. "If you ain't Calamity Jane Cannary I'm a son of a bitch. I'm Al Swearengen and I am the proprietor of this here establishment."

"It's a pleasure, Al. Call me Calam," I said. "Have we met before?"

"I hadn't had the pleasure," he replied. "But everyone knows you're the surest shot in the West – well, next to Wild Bill maybe. As I was coming down them steps I saw you hit that spittoon square-on at twenty feet. 'God damn' I says to myself. Not one pilgrim in twenty can hit the target like that. And not one gal in the whole West, excepting one. That's gotta be Calamity Jane. Jimmy, what's that silver dollar doing on the bar?"

"Miss Calam put it there to pay for her drinks."

Al picked up that fucking coin and handed it to me.

"You don't pay a fucking penny at the bar today, Little Lady. Jimmy, Miss Calam is my personal guest today. See that she gets whatever she wants. What are you drinking, Calam?"

I told him it was Old Potrero rye.

"Put a bottle of Old Potrero and a couple of glasses over on that cocksucking table, Jimmy. And put a fresh spittoon within shooting distance. Miss Calam and I are going to enjoy a drink or two together."

Al and I sat down at the table. He lit up a stogie and I took myself a new chaw.

The two of us sat there jawing and smoking and chewing and laughing until we got ourselves real familiar.

"How would you like to see one of our upstairs rooms?" he propositioned.

To tell the truth, I was real taken with Al Swearengen. I knew, running a place like the Gem, he was a whoremaster. And most whoremasters I'd run across were fucking assholes. But, I'll tell you right now. Al Swearengen is *not* a fucking asshole. And I'll knock anyone on his God damned ass who says he is.

I'd come to the Gem to find my husband. But Al's good looks and suave manner had me twitching in the coozy. I'd healed up from my romps with Deadwood Dick and figured I might just as well warm up the machinery with Al before giving Wild Bill his "Look, Sweetie, I'm back" fuck.

So Al and me staggered up the stairs to Whore Heaven, carrying what was left of the old Potrero with us. He opened one of the fuckrooms up there and shouted in.

"Alice, get your fucking ass out of there. Go down to the bar. Tell Jimmy to give you a couple of drinks on me. My friend here and me have a need for this here room right now."

A full bosomed redhead came out of the room, smiled at me, and hurried down the steps for her drinks on Whoremaster Al. I'll tell you, that man is all heart.

Once Alice was out of the room, Al locked the door and we got down to business.

.....

There's three kinds of fuckers in my book, the *expert*, the *inspired,* and the *everyday.*

Al Swearengen is an expert. As a whoremaster he hauls gals to his emporium from the East. Most of 'em are amateurs when he gets 'em to Deadwood. The professional ladies Back East in places like Buffalo and Alabama have their trade going and are living the life of

Riley. No need to come out here. It's gals that are down on their luck that Al takes pity on. He picks 'em up and hauls their asses here to the Black Hills. They get a new start in life and what with a hundred men to every woman eventually they find 'em a man, marry, and settle down. But at first, when they get brought out here to become upstairs girls, they have to learn to fuck. Not that they're virgins. Hell no. They've all been fucked, of course. But fucking for fun and fucking for money are two different things.

Al teaches 'em how to please a man fully and efficiently. So every technique ever invented by man has to be taught to the gals. Al has to fuck 'em and fuck 'em and fuck 'em until they get it right. Like I say, Al Swearengen is an *expert.*

Now a galoot like Deadwood Dick, he's what I call *inspired.* The way he fucks a gal comes from a natural inborn ability to vary his techniques and positions all the time. He didn't learn the ways of fucking like Al. He is just what I guess Madame Moustache would call an arteest. It's not at all like being fucked like an expert. So, like I say, Deadwood Dick is an *inspired* fucker.

Then, the third kind of fucker is the wham, bam, thank you ma'am kind. Like Wild Bill. It's nearly always the same old missionary, with him sometimes asking to have his cock sucked instead of or in addition to. It's nothing special. But if you love the guy like I loved Wild Bill Hickok, an *everyday* fuck is mighty satisfying, too.

In that fuckroom, Al fucked me every way from Sunday, I'll tell you. When Big Al finishes fucking you, you *know* you've been done up brown. His hands, fingers, mouth, tongue, cock and balls too, are doing every opening you got and few you didn't even know you had.

But unlike being fucked by an *inspired* type like Deadwood Dick, none of your holes are sore and tender afterwards. Why? Because Al never wants to bruise the merchandise. A whoremaster cares about keeping the girls operative same as a bullwhacker is careful never to let his blacksnake ever nip the skin of an ox. There's a name for that I heard oncet. It's *expertise.*

. . . . .

When Al had fucked me good and sound we finished off the bottle of rye and were happy as a couple of fucking bedbugs.

We step outta the room and go back downstairs when who do

you think we run into in the hall? None other than Wild Bill Hickok and a blonde with tits that just about burst outta her blouse. Jesus! I'd like to nuzzle into them myself. But I never got the chance to what with one thing and another. I just might hie me over to the Gem later and get me some of that now that I think of it.

"Calam!" Bill exclaimed. "I'll be fucked! It's great to have you in Deadwood. Meet my friend Clementine."

Clementine and I made nice with each other.

Bill spoke to Al.

"Al," he says. "Calam and I are old friends from way back. Would it be all right with you if me and her were to use that room Clementine and me just vacated?"

Al told us to be his guest. Al took Clementine by the hand and led her into the room he and I had just used so joyfully. Bill and I went into the room he'd just left.

It turned out that both those boys were up to at least one more fuck session. One thing I can say for old Bill and old Al. They sure as shit got stamina.

And speaking of stamina. My mouth has been running along here like a rattlesnake over a hot rock. I could sure use a little drink to soothe it some. Why, thank ye. Don't mind joining you in a little snort.

. . . . .

After what Al called our little swar-aye, he and Bill and me went downstairs for cocktails. Cocktails – that's the name Wild Bill was saying at the time to mean booze. It's an expression he picked up Back East when he was acting the part of himself in Buffalo Bill's theatrical productions. Al sent Alice back up the stairs to the fuckroom. He'd left Clementine up there to tidy up for the next customer.

When we'd done our cocktails, Bill and me headed back to camp. When we got there we were both plum tuckered out. All that drinking and fucking can kind of wear a body down. Charlie was zonked out in "my" tent when we got there. There was a pretty mining boy stretched out beside him. Both of 'em were buck-ass naked.

Charlie opened one eye when I peeked in.

"Howdy, Calam," he muttered.

"How've you been doing?" I asked him.

"Timmy and me been fucking," Charlie said. "How 'bout you?"

"Bill and me and Al and Clementine – we all been fucking, too," I advised him.

"Good for all four of you fuckers," he said.

"Give Timmy a kiss for me, you old cocksucker," I slurred.

Charlie kissed his companion.

"You got me dead to rights, Calam. Now go away. I need some more shuteye."

"Me too," I told him.

When I got to "Bill's" tent he was already sawing away.

I dropped into the bedroll and must have been dead to the world in less than half a minute.

. . . . .

Bill and me and Charlie slept the afternoon away. When Bill and me got to moving again I checked with Charlie. His companion, Timmy, had gone away somewhere.

"Come on, you two," Bill said to Charlie and me. "We've got to go find us some grub. I could eat a horse."

"Only one place to go for the best food in town," Charlie said.

"Where's that?" I asked.

Together the two boys said "Chinatown."

So we lit out for the lower end of Deadwood Gulch which houses the largest Chinatown east of Frisco.

. . . . .

The Badlands begin at the fork of Main and Sherman, in case you hadn't noticed. Keep a-going and you're in Chinatown, home to somewhere between a hundred and fifty to two hundred Celestials. Laundries, eateries, cheap bars, whorehouses, and opium dens are just *some* of what goes on down there. How do I know? I've checked most of 'em out.

Charlie led us direct to The Fat Eatery. Sam Fat is the guy who owns and operates it. He thought up the name as a kind of joke and it works. Because eventually everyone in town jokes about "the Fat Eatery." Then they go down to try it. And, by God, the fucking place can't be beat.

Sam Fat greeted us using an atrocious Chinese accent.

"Oh, Mistah Wild Bill, Mistah Colorlado, come in, come in. Who the charming companion, huh?"

I was introduced to our host.

"Oh, much pleasure, Miss Calamity. Please sit at best table, over here."

The "Best" table was in a rather dark corner. The kind Wild Bill favors, where he can sit with his back to the wall facing anyone who enters and where the shadows make him hard to see.

"What's your special tonight, Mister Sam?" Charlie asked in the most respectful tone possible.

"Loast pork, velly good. You get pork, mashed potato, gravy, peas, carrot, coffee, pie. Fifteen cents. Velly cheap. Velly good."

A meal like that could cost you over a quarter up in the gulch. But I knew Bill and Charlie had eaten here before so the eating was bound to be good. We ordered the special.

. . . . .

Charlie and Bill and me got to yakking. Charlie and Bill were pardners back in '68 in Hays running a freighting business. Back in Cheyenne they'd talked about maybe doing some freighting in Deadwood once they got here. And now, the two were discussing setting up a stage line or a pony express between Deadwood and Fort Laramie. I know that stretch pretty well. I'd driven an oxteam from Cheyenne through Fort Laramie and then up to Lusk, back and forth three times a few years back. I knew the lay of the land better than either Bill or Charlie.

We were just getting really into the discussion when Mister Sam brought on the grub.

Let me tell you, Stranger. You want to fill your God damned belly, you get your ass down there to Chinatown. That pork was the tenderest, sweetest, tastiest pig you ever want to flap a lip over. And them 'taters? Jesus Christ! Enough to make you cream your pants. My drawers are getting all warm and wet just thinking of them 'taters.

Mister Sam set a full coffeepot on the table, too.

Bill, Charlie and me gave our voices a rest and laid into that food. Like I said, you could pay a quarter or more up here in this part of town and not eat as well.

Bill's eyes, like always, was taking in everything in the room. But you wouldn't of knowed it. How he did that – observing everything while apparently observing nothing – is what kept him alive so long. The man who'd plugged so many sons of bitches had toted up a powerful lot of enemies out to get his ass. Those steely blue eyes, looking at nothing but seeing everything were as important to him as his quick draw and sure aim.

I saw Bill give a nudge of the elbow to Colorado Charlie. Neither Charlie or me are as good as Bill at seeing without looking. But we were a Hell of a lot better at it than your average cocksucker.

Bill and Charlie and me chewed our pork mighty quiet. Six of the best ears in the West were tuned to where the newcomer and our host were talking quietly.

I heard enough to realize that Sam Fat spoke English with an accent all right. An English accent. But I didn't catch the drift of the conversation. Charlie caught two important words he told us about later. They were *Tom Ng*. If he'd of told me the words then, they wouldn't of meant fuck-shit to me.

The stranger and Mister Sam stepped into the kitchen and out of hearing range.

"Who was *that* fucker?" I asked.

"The number one son of a bitch cocksucker in Deadwood," Charlie told me.

"Has the prick got a name?" I asked.

"Seth Bullock," Bill hissed.

"And how come Sam Fat can speak English without that coolie accent?"

"Back in China," Charlie explained, "he went to an English missionary school. He talks better English than you or me. He puts on that accent shit to give atmosphere to this joint."

"Okay," I said. "That explains that. Now tell me about the Bullock shithead."

"After we're outta here," Bill whispered. "I'm not sure we should talk about it here."

Before long, Sam Fat came shuffling back into the room. Seth Bullock must of gone out the back way.

"You likee food, huh? Good pork, good potato. What kind pie you want – we got apple," he said in that phoney Chinese accent of his which was supposed to give "flavor" to the joint.

We all told him we'd take apple.

He returned with apple pie slices and a fresh pot of coffee.

We thanked Mister Sam as we left his establishment and headed for the Little Bonanza Saloon to wet our whistles and talk about just who that son of a fucking bitch Seth Bullock was.

.....

Little Bonanza was a good choice. It don't have whores or gambling tables. It don't have a stage or dancing girls. It don't serve meals or free lunch. What it's got is booze and quiet.

The Little Bonanza is pure and simple a drinking establishment. Pete Carson who runs the place is big, strong, and dour. He don't allow no loud talk or brawls and he's his own bouncer. Just the place for a quiet talk among friends.

Bill got a bottle of Old Crow and three glasses and brought 'em to a corner table where he could have his back to two walls.

As we settled into some serious drinking, Bill and Charlie told me about that cocksucker Bullock. What it amounted to is that the crooks in town made Bullock sheriff. Bullock's in cahoots with every slimebag in town and uses his position to protect the crooks and cover up his own shady dealings. When Bill came to town, Seth Bullock was afraid he'd try to take over as lawman. So he hated Bill.

"What do you suppose he was doing in Chinatown?" I asked.

"I caught two important words in his conversation with Sam Fat," Charlie said. "They were Tom Ng. Tom Ng is the head of the criminal element in Chinatown. Sam Fat is respected by both the honest tong and the criminal one. If Seth is trying to get in touch with the elusive Tom Ng, he's up to no fucking good."

I'd only been in Deadwood one day and I already knew who the bad guys were in town. Their names were Seth Bullock and Tom Ng.

Bill and Charlie and me were sick of talking about those assholes. So we settled down to some serious drinking.

And thinking of drinking, anyone around here up for a little nip? Well, thank you, barkeep. Don't mind if I do.

.....

The next morning when I woke up, Bill was already gone. Charlie had a campfire going with a pot of coffee and a frying pan with bacon sizzling in it.

"I'm about to fry me a couple of eggs. Would you like a couple yourself, Calam?" he asked.

"Wouldn't hurt none," I told him as I poured myself a cup of his strong boiled coffee.

"What time is it?" I asked him.

Charlie hauled his big watch outta his pocket.

"Right close to noon, Calam."

"Jesus!" I said. "We really tied one on last night, didn't we?"

"Yep," Charlie answered, breaking four eggs into the frying pan where that bacon was sending out odors to get the old appetite whetted.

"Tied one on last night, the night afore, and the night afore that. I'm a-hoping we'll tie one on tomorrow night, the next one, and the next one. Fucking and drinking. Drinking and fucking. Won't be long afore I have my stage and freight line running between here and Fort Laramie. Then I'll have to cut back on how pie-eyed I get at night."

Now *that* was a sobering thought. So I went into the tent and brought out a bottle. I laced my coffee with a hefty shot of rye. It improved Charlie's coffee a lot.

"Where's Bill?" I asked.

"He got up over an hour ago," Charlie answered. "Headed down to the bathhouse. I'll be doing the same after I get down some breakfast."

I swear. Wild Bill Hickok and Colorado Charlie Utter have got to have been the cleanest pilgrims in the West. Bathed their fucking hides every day they weren't on the trail. And even then, if there was a river or creek, they was in it in the morning.

Charlie pushed a couple of eggs and some bacon onto a tin plate for me and ate his eggs and bacon outta the frying pan Colorado style.

"Did Bill come back from the bathhouse with his dirties?" I asked.

"Naw. He said he was going to leave 'em with the Celestial there at the bathhouse. The Celestial'll haul 'em down to Ah-Chin for a nickel. Bill thought he'd try that out today."

We ate in silence. Charlie sweetened up his coffee with some of the whiskey I'd brought out.

"Do you know where Bill was going after his bath, Charlie?" I asked as I hauled out an after-breakfast chaw.

"He said Shingle's Number Three Saloon," Charlie told me.

"There's three or four saloons he goes to to gamble. Likes to move around among 'em so's no one will know for sure where he is at any time. You know how he is."

Yep. I knew how Wild Bill was. Always aware there were motherfuckers out to get him. Fuckers like that "sheriff" Seth Bullock. And the hills were full of others who were unknown cocksuckers who'd like to murder him just to be able to say they killed Wild Bill Hickok.

No one could out-draw my Bill. What he had to guard against was some shithead who'd know where he was going to be so's they could ambush him. Cowardly cocksuckers!

I'd finished my breakfast and spit a wad of 'baccy in the fire. Charlie lit up one of his clay pipes and puffed away while swilling down his coffee and rye. We sat there by the fire with contented bellies just watching the fire die down.

You know I ain't a cleanliness freak like Bill and Charlie. So when I'd finished off my chaw 'stead of heading for the bathhouse I planned to go find Shingle's Number Three. I knew Charlie would clean up my tin plate and fork and cup. He never let anyone else clean up the plates and pans and stuff after a meal he'd cooked. Like I say, he's a real stickler for cleanliness.

Charlie told me how to find the saloon and I headed up to Main Street to see how Wild Bill was doing at the table.

Number Three was pretty easy to find. I stepped inside and looked around. A decent sized bar, fuckroom up the stairs, a cashier's cage at the far wall, and three poker tables. No stage to distract the players. The table over in the corner was pretty much in shadows. Bill's kind of gambling hell.

As always, I looked at where Bill was without really eyeing it. He saw me come in, and no one would ever know he'd seen me. We never, ever, acknowledged each other in public.

I sauntered up to the bar and ordered two fingers of whatever rye the house whiskey was.

. . . . .

Behind the bar there was a real bruiser. I judged him to be about three hundred pounds. But all that weight appeared to be pure bone and muscle. And the muscles that showed beneath his shirt and vest were nothing if not powerful. This was a man to reckon with.

He had a shaved head, a shaved face (no beard) and a smile that showed absolute self-assurance. This pilgrim was not only a barkeep. He served as bouncer and general peacekeeper. No shit was going down in this joint while *this* guy was tending the place.

He set my rye down on the bar.

"Welcome to the Number Three," he said.

I slid a buck onto the bar next to the shot. He pushed it back.

"For a fine lady like yourself, the first drink's on me," he said in a way that made my coozy twitch. Here was a man who could get anything he wanted from any real woman with no more than a soft word, a smile, and rippling muscles.

"Fine lady, indeed," I thought. No one would ever dare call me fine. Except this hunk of solid manliness.

"Thanks, pardner," I said.

"You're welcome," he smiled. "I'm Dusty Rhodes. I don't own this here place, but I run it. If you're looking for a saloon where there's peace and quiet, drop in any time. The only joint in town where there's drinking, gambling, and fucking, with no fights, arguments, brawls, or disorderly conduct."

"I'll remember that," I told him.

I extended my hand. "My name's Jane. Pleased to meet you, Dusty."

He shook my hand, looked over the table where Bill was sitting, and winked.

That wink spoke volumes. It showed me he knew who I was and that I was connected to Wild Bill Hickok. It also told me he would keep all that knowledge to himself. I could be just "Plain Jane from the Plains" in Shingle's Number Three. No questions asked.

I downed my drink and ordered another. I shoved the silver dollar on the bar. He let it sit this time. He would let me use up the dollar in drinks now. I liked that.

I took me a chaw of 'baccy while Dusty set up a two-fingered shot of better than average rye on the bar.

Dusty went down to t'other end of the bar and busied himself with polishing some glasses.

I'd placed myself so there was a spittoon between me and Bill's table. I turned away from the bar and aimed a glob at that spittoon. Hot fucking damn! Hit 'er fair and square. I stole a look at the gambling table while my glob was in the air.

Let me tell you how the gambling table was set up. Bill's chair was in the far corner, with his back to two walls. In other words, his preferred spot. Wherever Bill sat, that was twelve o'clock.

The player at ten o'clock had his back to me. He was holding his cards away from his vest, so I could glimpse at his hand. Young guy, black hair. That's all I could tell about him, other than that he had a pair of sevens.

To his right, at nine o'clock, was a well dressed paper collar, balding, middle-aged guy holding his cards close to the vest.

I turned away from the table after hitting the fucking spittoon. I lifted my shot glass with my left hand. Bill knew from that that ten o'clock had a pair of something. If I'd lifted the glass with my right hand it would have meant I'd spotted three of a kind. When Bill was dealing he knew what the other players were holding. In this case he wasn't dealing and knowing just the information I'd telegraphed to him gave him a slight advantage. Bill had the mind of an excellent scout. He could assemble tiny bits of information into a pattern that helped him track a varmint or win a buck from a stranger.

With my well-developed hearing I could pick up what was going on at Bill's table. The kid at ten o'clock was losing something fierce. That meant Bill was doing his God damnedest to use his card mechanic skills and my signals to help the fucker win. It was bad for business to have a sucker leave the table pissed off. But the God damned sucker was such a shitty player he kept on losing even with Bill cheating to help him. What can you do with a dumb motherfucker like that?

I heard the fucker say, "God damn it to Hell. That wipes me out."

Dusty came ambling down towards my end of the bar to pour me another shot. But his attention was directed more to the gambling table than to the pouring of the booze. I knew that if the loser raised his voice any higher, or even if he didn't just shut the fuck up, his ass would be out the door in seconds.

Bill's answer to the kid was soft and calm. But audible.

"Look, Son, he said. "Here's ten bucks. Go over there to the bar and have yourself a drink on me."

Hell! Those ten bucks would buy not one drink but a shitload of booze.

"No, siree," the kid answered. "I don't take charity from nobody."

Dusty was close to moving in on the situation. Ugly rumblings are not allowed at Shingle's Number Three.

Bill answered the young loser in his most soothing voice.

"It ain't charity, Son. You've had a mean streak of shitty luck. It can happen to anyone, including me. So, sometime when you and me are at a table and Lady Luck is pissing all over me, I expect you to give me ten bucks from your winnings and I'll have a drink on you. Then we'll be even."

The fucking loser grabbed the ten bucks without so much as a "thank you."

The paper collar who'd been sitting at nine o'clock tapped him on the shoulder and said, "You've been taken, Lad."

The paper collar got up from the table himself and went over to the cage and cashed in his chips. He patted the young chump on the shoulder and marched outta the saloon.

The shitty young player who'd lost it all at the table came shuffling up to where I was at the bar.

. . . . .

Now one of the things I'm really good at is making a man feel good. I wanted to cheer the fucker up and decrease the venom he was feeling. Bill's ten dollar bill hadn't quieted the asshole enough to water down the hatred.

So when he got up to the bar I greeted him.

"Howdy, Pilgrim. You look like you could use some cheering up. How 'bout letting a lady buy you a drink?"

Dusty was right there behind the bar ready to take an order.

"I don't let dames buy me drinks," the loser grumbled.

"Suit yourself," I said with a smile. "That's right chivalrous of you. It's always nice to meet a gentleman."

That kinda changed his mood a bit.

"How's 'bout I buy *you* a drink, Young Lady," he smiled.

His smile somehow reminded me of the way a rat might look if it was trying to be polite.

I looked him up and down, making an eye-stop at where there should've been a bulge in his jeans on the way down and on the way up.

Most guys like that, and this chump was no exception.

"Tell you what," I answered. "I can see you're a sporting man." I took another fixed gander at his crotch. "And I happen to like a sporting man. How 'bout we roll the dice? Low man treats."

Although he'd just lost big he seemed to like the idea that he came across as a sport.

"Sure," he said. "I'll shoot you for drinks."

"Agreed," I said. "Shake, Pard. My name's Jane."

"Jack," he answered. shaking my hand. "Jack McCall. Always happy to be of service to a lady."

"Hey, Dusty," I said. "Would there happen to be a pair of dice in the joint?"

Dusty poured drinks for me and Jack, and set a pair of dice on the bar with the drinks. Most barkeeps in Deadwood keep dice behind the bar.

Shooting for drinks is one of the most prevalent sports in town.

Me and Jack stood there and shot the dice and shot the shit for well over an hour. I offered him a chaw. Me and him drank and chewed and jawed and spit as the sap's tongue got looser and looser and his aim at the spittoon got worser and worser.

His lies got more monstrous as he got drunker. He told me he'd been a big time cattle rustler. Then that he was feared far and wide as a desperado. Bull shit! The more he boasted the more he showed what a pathetic asshole he really was.

He veered between being a braggart and crying in his booze. In his sad mood he told me about his loss at the poker table.

"Yeah," he said. "I got wiped out by that cocksucker sitting in the corner. I'm a Hell of a great poker player, myself. I don't see how I could lose so fast in a game that was fair and square."

"From the way you roll those dice," I told him, "I can see that you are a Hell of a gambler."

That was the truth. He wasn't even very good at throwing the fucking dice. But he took what I said the way I meant him to take it. As if I thought he was hot shit.

"Yeah," he replied. "I *am* a Hell of a gambler. That guy who was sitting next to me at the table. He's Moccasin Varner?"

"The paper collar?" I asked.

"That's the guy. A real big shot here in town. Owns the X-10-U-8 restaurant down the street. Also owns the EQ Stables. I'm his number one man. He staked me to that poker game over there. So now I've not only lost my wad, I owe Moccasin for my stake to boot."

There ain't nothing more pitiful than a lying drunk who gets to feeling sorry for hisself. So I steered him back to lying abut his exploits as a rustler and desperado. And then to how fucking clever he was as his boss'"number one" man. I guessed that he washed dishes at Varner's restaurant and shoveled shit at his stable. I had Colorado Charlie check that out for me the next day. Turned out I was dead-on right.

When the lying cocksucker was pie-eyed enough, me and him staggered outta the Number Three and headed across the creek to my tent.

I was a lot steadier on my feet than Jack, which was a good thing. He wouldn't have made it to the tent without a lot of support from me.

Once inside my tent, the fucker dropped onto my bedroll. He hadn't passed out, so I decided to try to show him a good time. I wanted him to feel good enough about the day so he wouldn't have a hardon against Wild Bill.

"You wanna have yourself a grand old time, Jack?" I asked him.

"Yeah," he muttered. "Let's fuck. I'm probably the greatest lover in Deadwood."

He couldn't say it without slobbering all over his scraggly beard.

"Let's see what you've got, Big Boy," I coaxed.

He made a feeble attempt to unbuckle his belt, but he didn't have enough concentration to get the task done.

"Here, Jack. Let me get this son of a bitch off," I told him as I got his belt off and his pants unbuttoned. He just laid there giggling like a bitch.

I unbuttoned the bottom buttons of his union suit. And Jesus Christ Almighty! I was confronted with the tiniest prick I've ever seen.

You know, I've seen hundreds of pricks in my time. You could say that cocks and cunts are my lifetime hobby. Sometimes big men have little peckers and little men have big peckers. You never know. But here was a little son of a bitch with a teeny-weeny prick. Like I say. You never know.

I started to work that pathetic little peter to try to get it hard. I handled it. I stroked it. I licked it. I sucked it. Nothing! It just laid there, not worth a shit.

The asshole was too out of it to respond. Well, it wasn't much of a dick anyway. So's I didn't feel I'd missed nothing. The bastard passed out while I had his dong in my mouth and he had the nerve to snore something awful.

. . . . .

I stood up and looked at him. A little man with a little cock. Couldn't play poker worth a shit. Poorest damned liar I'd met in a long time.

Pathetic cocksucker!

I bit me off a chaw and spit it in his face. He didn't so much as flinch.

I branded him with that glob. Loser!

What I couldn't know at the time, though, was this. That son of a bitching cocksucking asshole who was snoring on my bed with my 'baccy juice smeared on his face and his pathetic pecker hanging out, would, in exactly two weeks to the day, and nearly to the hour, shoot and kill my husband, Wild Bill Hickok.

It's enough to make me puke, just thinking about it. Man, could I ever use a drink. Well, thank you, Pard. Don't mind if I do.

Chapter Three

THE RETURN OF DEADWOOD DICK

I took me a walk around town to get the taste of that little fucker out of my mouth. When I got back to my tent, he was gone. I learned later that Colorado Charlie had stopped by, seen the son of a bitch, hauled his ass out of the tent and dragged him down to the bathhouse. He paid the Celestial to carry Jack, just as he was, to Chinatown and leave him there with his dick hanging out, 'baccy juice all over his face, and slobber drooling out of his mouth, for everyone to look at. From what I hear, Jack drew quite a crowd.

That was all before he did the dirty deed, of course. I would get revenge on him for that later. I'll tell you about it sometime.

.....

The next morning, Bill and Charlie and me went out to the IXL eatery next to the Bella Union for breakfast. The breakfast menu is always the same. For twenty cents, you can get slapjacks, beans, bacon, and coffee. So, that's what we ordered. The thing about the breakfast at the IXL is, you can go back for seconds, and thirds and fourths as much as you want. And for anything, beans, bacon, slapjacks, coffee. And the three of us took 'em up on that big time.

The food was no better than we could've whumped up back at camp. But Bill wanted breakfast out, so that's what we did.

When we'd stuffed our gullets to where we would've gagged on another bite we kicked back with our fifth coffee refill to shoot the shit.

"O.K. Pard," Charlie said, patting his belly. "You've brought us here for a reason. I know an occasion when I see one. What is it *this* time?"

Wild Bill gave Charlie that cold stare that sometimes meant he was about to shoot you or about to laugh. You couldn't judge what was on Bill's mind by the steadiness of that gaze. Since Charlie and me knew Bill wasn't gonna draw, we guessed that a laugh would follow. It did.

"God damn, Charlie," he chortled. "There are only two people in the world who can read me like that. And you're one of 'em."

"Who the fuck's t'other one?" I asked.

"I'm not gonna tell you, Calam," he answered. "Cause if I did, you'd get the big head. And you're conceited enough as it is."

We all laughed hard enough to draw the attention of the other customers of the IXL. Shit! Drawing attention never bothered any of us none. It's what we did without trying.

When we got done laughing, Colorado Charlie picked up where he left off. I swear to God. That man is the most persistent son of a bitch I ever knew. Once he gets on the trail of something he never gives up. That makes him a Hell of a good guy to have on your side. He might be queer as fools' gold. But, by damn, he's the most faithful friend Bill or me ever had.

"C'mon, Pard," he said. "Give! Why the fuck are we here stuffing our yobs instead of eating my good cooking back in camp?"

"I thought you'd never ask," Bill said. And we all laughed again.

Bill took time to light a stogie. Charlie stuffed one of his clay pipes with 'baccy and borrowed a light from Wild Bill. I took me a chaw.

"Since we got here to Deadwood," Bill said. "Lady Luck has been showering me with sweet loving."

Charlie and me knew Bill's card mechanic skills had more to do with his "luck" than Chance did. But we held our God damned tongues.

"So," Bill went on. "I've gathered enough money to be able to invest in the freighting business again, Charlie. Like we ran that business back in Hays in sixty-nine."

Charlie didn't show no emotion. Bill and Charlie had gone over all this before we left Cheyenne. They were simply in a holding position until Charlie had checked out the possibilities and Bill had raised the moolah.

"That's good, Bill," was all Charlie said. But I knew from the way Bill set his broad shoulders there was more to come.

"Yes, Bill," I pushed. "That's great. What more are you gonna tell us?"

Bill allowed himself a tiny smile behind his moustaches.

"I think it's time to move," he told us.

"Wait a moment," Charlie said. "Just one fucking moment. The whole idea was that we were gonna set up a freight line, and maybe even a passenger line, from Deadwood to Fort Laramie. Now that we're here in Deadwood you announce we're gonna move?"

"Not outta Deadwood, Charlie," Bill said calmly. "Outta the God damned tents. I not only have enough stash to finance the business. There's enough to boot to move the three of us to the Overland Hotel."

Colorado Charlie made it his business to know everything going on in town.

"The Overland, huh?" he questioned. "Pretty fancy. Twenty-six rooms and a stove in every fucking room. Two different parlors for relaxing. No bars or whores. Keeps out the drunks and riffraff. I know the place, Bill. How much is the owner, Squinty Bartles, asking for the rooms you're thinking of?"

"Twenty bucks a week per room," Bill said. "We'll need two rooms. Five dollars more for a second person in a room."

"Then we're talking about forty-five bucks a week." Charlie reckoned. "They gonna board us as well as room us for that?"

"Nope," Bill said. "Rooms only."

"Jesus Christ," I said. "We really got enough to pay that and take all our meals out?"

Bill just gave me that steely-eyed glare for an answer. I knew that meant Wild Bill had his poke jam-full of pickings from the tables in the gambling hells he'd spent so much time in.

After Bill'd paid for our breakfast we marched ourselves right over to the hotel.

. . . . .

Bill paid Bartles in advance for the two rooms, one for him and Charlie and one for me. Which, like you've already figured out, would end up one room for Bill and me and the next door one for Charlie. Bill never did allow to the world that me and him were married and bedding down together at night. Like I told you afore, we didn't want nothing to stand in the way of his skirt chasing and my everlasting hunt for new cock and cunt.

We went upstairs to check out the rooms. The Overland was the newest and the finest hotel in town. Those rooms were as nice as any I'd seen anywhere. Looked like easy living to me.

Bill and Charlie thought it would look best if they were to break camp without me. So I went over to the Gem for a few drinks while they took down our two tents, packed up our gear, and stored the whole God damned kit and caboodle, except for the stuff we would need while living at the Overland, in Chinatown at Ah-Chin's Laundry and Storage Depot.

And while my pards were doing that, I was entertaining the folks at the Gem with my stories about how I'd chased Jesse James and his gang all over Missouri. And how I'd done old Jesse himself. Those barflies kept buying me drinks and I just couldn't stop 'em from doing so.

I guess some folks know it's polite to treat a lady to a drink if she's entertaining you with her gab. Well, thank you, Pilgrim.

. . . . .

Me and Bill and Charlie moved into the two rooms at the Overland that very afternoon. It wasn't that any of us needed the comfort of a hotel room. Hell, we'd been cozy as flies on a turd in those two tents down by the creek. But recently, Bill had been appearing kinda moody, and was even a little grumpy for him. The move to Main Street, I think, was more a reaction to his pissanty mood than anything else.

After we'd put our things away in the rooms, we went out to eat at the X-10-U-8 eatery. The one owned by Johnny "Mocassin" Varnes.

I'd told Bill and Charlie everything Jack McCall had told me at the bar at Single's Number Three. So they knew that the two men who'd left the gambling table pissed off at Bill were associated with the X-10-U-8. One of 'em, the owner, the other a flunky. I never asked, but I figured out we were going to that particular eating place to get a feel for the two losers in their own cage. We didn't spot either of 'em there. I guess it wasn't time yet for the showdown that had to come.

After our meal, we went back to the Overland to sit in one of the parlors and enjoy our 'baccy.

Bill was looking kinda down in the mouth as he sat on a yellow sofa and puffed on his stogie.

"You're looking right thoughtful, Pard," Charlie told him. "Is something biting at your nuts?"

"I'll tell you, Charlie and Calam," Bill said. "I'm convinced Deadwood is my last camp."

"You mean you're planning on settling down here permanent like?" Charlie asked.

"Real permanent," Bill said in tones that sent fucking chills up my spine.

"Come on, Wild Bill," I piped up. "You don't think you're in any more danger here than anywhere else, do you?"

"I think 'it' is here," was what he had to say.

Me and Charlie knew what he meant by "it." We'd heard him say about a thousand times, "The bullet hasn't been made that can kill Wild Bill Hickok." He never had feared death because he was convinced he led a charmed life.

"If the bullet with your name on it is here in Deadwood," Charlie said. "Then let's get us the fuck outta town."

"No," Bill said very definitely. "Deep in my gut I've go a hunch I'll never leave this gulch alive."

"Do you think it's that asshole Seth Bullock, the so-called sheriff, who's got the God damned bullet in his gun?" Charlie asked.

I'd had the same fucking suspicion of Bullock. He hated Wild Bill. He was afraid Bill would take that tin star off his vest.

"I don't reckon Bullock's got the balls," Bill answered. "Could be he's got the God damned bullet. But somehow I don't feel so."

I spit a gob into the spittoon. I was so wrought up I nearly missed it. There weren't no 'baccy stains on the carpet yet, so I was glad I wasn't gonna the first one to dye it brown.

We didn't discuss the matter further. Seemed like everything'd been said that needed saying.

.....

I remembered hearing there was a female faro dealer at Jim Persate's Wild West Saloon called Madame Moustache. Phatty Thompson'd told me she was good at three things, faro dealing, cock sucking, and spiritualizing.

I didn't know then, and I don't know now, if I believe in God damned ghosts. But I'd promised myself back when I was riding in Phatty's wagon I'd see if this arteest, Madame Moustache, could lick a cunt as good as she could suck a dick.

I planned to go see her the next day at Jim Persate's. It's down at the corner of Main and Gold Streets. I don't play faro, but I like to have my button rung. And maybe, just maybe, I could find out from the spirits whether "it" had really been made, and, if so, whether it was in Deadwood.

.....

I didn't get around to checking out the Wild West Saloon until mid-afternoon the next day. Since I'd come to town, I'd toured a shitload of saloons already. But with seventy-five watering holes in town, I'd only skimmed the surface. I'd been saving the Wild West to scout when or if I got horny for a good cunt-suck. From what Phatty had told me on our wagon-trip, Madame Moustache was likely to give me first class service. And now I had a double purpose in looking her up. If she was as good a spiritualizer as she was a cock sucker, maybe the spooks she consorted with would know whether the bullet with Wild Bill Hickok's name on it had been manufactured yet. And, if so, whether it was here in this shithole of a town.

As soon as I entered the Wild West I figured out exactly what kind of a sucker joint it was. Instead of being a gambling hell where the player has a decent chance of winning, it was rigged heavily for the house.

First clue was that the poker tables were few and far between. The games that were featured were blackjack and faro, games where the dealer, who is in the best position to cheat, is an employee of the hell.

Wild Bill would never gamble at any table where he couldn't control the game and cheat. That eliminated faro and blackjack. He never saw any reason to gamble at anything, even his gambling on life and death, unless the odds were on his side. That's why, for so many years, he never lost at poker or at quick-draw. The money he won and the men he killed proved that he always had the advantage. That is, until August second, 1876. I'll tell you how and why he lost more than money that day. But not right now. I want to tell you about my meeting with Madame Moustache at the Wild West.

But first, I'd sure like to wet my whistle. Just thinking of Madame Moustache makes me think of good *rye whiskey. The piss they serve at the bar at the Wild West always gives me a craving for a shot of something decent like Old Potrero. Well, thank you, Stranger.*

.....

First off, I sidled up to the bar. The bar down there isn't friendly like this here one. No free welcoming drink on the house down there at the Wild West. Two bits'll get you a shot of watered-down moonshine. That should tell you something abut the shitty attitude towards us thirsty pilgrims. I downed the piss I was served, took a chaw, and ordered a second shot. It was pretty bad, but I've drunk worse. But not much worse.

With my second shot in hand, I moseyed about the God damned gambling hell doing target practice on every spittoon in the place. It was easy as shit to pick out Madame Moustache as I cased out every dealer on my wanderings.

There were three faro banks in the joint. Two of 'em had male cocksuckers as dealer/bankers. The third bank had a tiny woman with a dark moustache in charge. No question who *that* was.

If she tops five foot in height I'm a fucking shiteating cunt. Shit! She's still banking faro down there at Persate's. You can amble down there and see her for yourself. Even play the game at her table if you don't mind getting cheated at cards.

The only way for the house or the dealer to make any real money at faro is by cheating. In a really fair game, the house can't do better than break even. I knew from what Phatty had told me that the Madame had been run outta one mining camp after another out in Californy for double-dealing blackjack. Here in the Black Hills she'd changed her game from cheating at blackjack to cheating at faro.

Action was slow at the Wild West that afternoon. There weren't no gamblers at Madame Moustache's table. In order to get acquainted with her, I was gonna have to lose a few bucks at her table. I'd already agreed with myself that I'd havta let her take me for a while to warm her up afore I could tell her my proposition.

. . . . .

I approached Madame Moustache's table, which, as on all faro layouts, the thirteen cards of the spade suit are pasted down on the velvet I placed a quarter on the six and spit into the nearby spittoon as if for luck. I knew luck wouldn't have nothing to do with it, but I had to fucking pretend, didn't I?

The Madame had shuffled the deck in her hand and turned up a card, *soda*. She placed it to her left on the table. Soda has no bearing on the bets. It's simply a formality. She turned up the next card, the Jack of Hearts and placed it to the right. If anyone had place a bet on the jack on the table, he would have lost. She turned up the Three of Clubs next. Three of Clubs would have won.

My bet stayed on the table. Madame flipped the beads on her counting machine.

On the next turn, the third card was the Six of Diamonds. I won. I knew I'd win my first bet. That was to keep me in the game. I won the second turn, lost the third, and so it went. I lost just slightly more than I won. What added zest to game was that I couldn't catch her manipulating the cards. In my book, Madame Moustache is Wild Bill's near equal at cheating.

The Madame keeps up a clever line of chatter with the suckers.

"Where are you from?" "I've been there. Do you happen to know Joseph Potter? He was panning for gold there back in sixty-two," and so on.

Her French accent makes everything she says sound somehow more interesting than it really is.

I was about to start jawboning with her about my real reason for being there when, God damn it, a young miner came up to the table. I needed there to be just me and Madame Moustache to proposition her about a cunt-lick and a see-ounce.

The young cocksucker plunked a twenty dollar goldpiece on the ten. Madame laid down her three cards. On the third turn the fucking miner won. I knew he would. You know it too. That was supposed to keep the asshole at the table. Instead of staying as he was supposed to, he picked up his twenty dollar win and walked away. Big fucking mistake.

Madame Moustache had a little coughing fit. By the time the fit was over a big fucking bruiser came outta the woodwork somewhere. I turned to aim a wad of 'baccy juice at a spittoon that was in the direction of the door. I saw the cocksucking miner leave in a big fucking hurry. The bruiser wasn't more than three paces behind him.

I knew the miner learned an important lesson when the bruiser caught up with him outside. In a gambling hell like Jim Persate's Wild West, don't think you're gonna pull a fast one by taking advantage of the first "come-on" win.

.....

Now, with the cocksucker outta the way, I could let the Madame go on with her winning ways as I pushed into the real reason I was there.

"How's Fifi?" I asked.

That caught her unawares. I knew Phatty Thompson had given her at least one cat. Probably a couple. And one of the new cats she got was to replace her lost Fifi. So I felt pretty sure one of her new cats would get the prized name.

"Fifi?" Madame responded, testing me out.

"Your cat," I ventured.

"My Fifi is doing well," she smiled. "How do you happen to know the name of my dear little friend?"

"I'm a friend of Phatty Thompson," I told her. "I helped him bring his wagonload of cats to Deadwood. He told me to look you up. He says you are a very talented lady."

I won two-bits on the next turn of the cards.

"Which of my talents did he describe to you?" she asked.

"He said you are an arteest. That you can work wonders with your mouth and tongue. I would be interested in being one of your clients. That is, if they apply to members of my sex."

"For women like you, I have a special rate," she said.

"How much?"

"Twenty dollars."

"And what is your regular rate?" I asked her.

"Twenty dollars," she said.

We both laughed at that, but not loud enough to draw attention to ourselves.

"There's another specialty of yours Phatty told me about," I told her.

She raised her eyebrows as if to silently ask what I meant.

"He told me you do spiritualizing in see-ounces."

"We will talk about these things at a later time," she told me. "Meet me at midnight tonight at room twelve of the Grand Central Hotel. Be prepared to cross my palm with gold for the séance. The spirits will not divulge their secrets to misers."

. . . . .

I'd only lost two bucks total at the table. It was time to leave.

"I'll see you at midnight," I told her.

I tipped her a quarter and left the joint. I had gambled by the house rule. That is, I hadn't won at the table. So I knew I wouldn't be followed by the bruiser. I didn't just fall off the turnip cart.

Anyone around here getting thirsty by any chance? You are, Pardner? Sure, I'll join you.

. . . . .

I arrived at the Grand Central Hotel at midnight, as planned. Madame Moustache answered her door immediately after I knocked.

She was wearing a kind of bathrobe that she called a pen-war. It was very silky and, I guess, very French as well.

A fluffy white cat was moseying around the room. I asked her if that was Fifi. She picked the cat up and gave it a kiss. She introduced me to the damned thing. I like animals fine. But I'll be fucked before I'll ever kiss one. As a matter of fact, I *was* fucked by a grizzly oncet. I guess I already told you about that, though, didn't I?

Madame asked me if I would like a cup of tea. I'm not very big on tea, unless it's fortified with a shot of rye. But I was on my good behavior and said I'd be glad to join her. I didn't ask if she had a bottle of hooch to flavor it with.

She had a little kerosene stove lit with a pot of water already bubbling on it. She brewed the tea and we sat at a round table sipping the bitter tasting brew.

"Before we start the séance, I wonder if you have any questions you'd like to ask me," she said.

"Yeah," I told her. "For starters, do I call you Madame or what?"

"My name is Marie," she said. "I let people I like call me that and…I can tell you frankly, you are a person I like. I believe *your* name is Martha Hickok."

Holy shit! This lady was good! I didn't think anyone but Wild Bill and Colorado Charlie knew that was my legal name.

"Jean-Luc told me," she said.

"Who the fuck is Jon Luke?" I asked.

"He is the spirit with whom I communicate," she told me.

"Well Jon Luke is technically right on," I told her. "But what I go by is Calamity Jane. And my friends call me Calam."

"Then, since I hope I am your friend, I will call you Calam as well. And I will instruct Jean-Luc to use the name you prefer as well," she told me.

"That's fine and dandy with me," I said. "Now, this here Jon Luke, is he the only spook you talk to?"

"Yes. He is my guide," she said. "He was, and is, a great philosopher. He was killed during our French revolution."

Now *that* was a relief. I was worried that the spooks she was going to be meeting might include some of the men Wild Bill had plugged. I wouldn't want that. They might not have Wild Bill's best interests at heart.

"Am I going to be able to talk to this Jon Luke fucker myself?" I asked.

"I am afraid Jean-Luc's English is not very good. I will communicate with him and then he will communicate his answers in his own way."

"When do we start?" I asked.

"Immediately, if you wish," she answered.

She cleared the table and brought over a velvet table cloth with some weird figures on it that I couldn't make ass or elbow out of. She placed a spirit lamp on it that she lit. It kinda sputtered but threw out a faint glow.

She turned off the gaslamps on the wall so our only light was from the sputtering fucker on the table.

"Jean-Luc was a disciple of Jean-Jacques Rousseau," she told me.

That didn't ring no bells with me.

"He believes we communicate best in a state of nature. So the séance will work best if we divest ourselves of our garments."

"You mean we're gonna get buck-ass naked?" I asked.

She nodded.

"Hot damn!" I said. "I can tell I'm gonna really like this see-ounce."

She shed the bathrobe and I hopped outta my clothes in a jiffy, leaving my pants close beside me so I could get to the pockets. I knew the score.

Marie had a nice, perky set of titties. She had the thickest black bush I've ever seen. I guess I wasn't too surprised that a lady with a moustache might be pretty heavily forested in her twat-triangle.

She took me in with an approving eye, too. I figured that the two of us might have ourselves one Hell of a time once the see-ounce was over.

We sat at the table, facing each other tit to boob in the flickering light.

"Before I call upon Jean-Luc to appear, I need you to cross my palm with gold."

I reached down to the floor where my pants were and hauled out a twenty dollar goldpiece. I made a cross with it on her hand which was lying on the table. Her fingers encircled the coin and it disappeared before my very eyes. Shit almighty! The French doll was *good*!

She began speaking in a foreign language. Must have been French. It was in a singsong.

"Gaze into the flame," she said after she'd mumbled in that language for a couple of minutes.

I looked at the flame and she picked up her mumbo-jumbo again. Damned if I could keep my eyes open. I'd open 'em, close 'em, open 'em, close 'em. I wondered if she'd slipped something into my tea. I was feeling weird. Good, but weird.

"Jean-Luc is in the room with us now, Calam. Can you feel his presence?"

"Your damned tootin I can," I answered.

I felt chills running up and down my spine, and I sensed a sweet smell in the air that hadn't been there before.

"Jean-Luc is prepared to answer any questions you care to put to him. Are you ready to ask?"

"Hell, yes," I said. "Ask him if 'it' has been made yet."

"Keep your focus on the flame," she told me. "Jean-Luc will give your answer there. But you must think of nothing but your quest. Whatever 'it' is, concentrate only on that."

She went into that weird chanting sound again that was like to spook me outta my fucking skin. I stared at the damned flame as hard as I could. I concentrated on the thought of the God damned bullet. Had it been made yet? Her mumbling sounds buzzed through my head. The flame turned from one color to another. My fucking eyes could barely stay open. All I could think of was the God damned bullet. Has the bullet been made? Has the bullet been made? Has the bullet been made? Has the…

Holy fucking shit! The flame turned purple. And right there in that purple flame I saw… No! God damn it! Yes! Oh, fuck!

What I saw through my bleary eyes was a cartridge. My eyes were watering something fierce, but I focused all my attention on the fucking bullet. There was writing engraved right into it. Tiny letters. I strained to read what it said. Then, I made out the name inscribed on the fucker.

Wild Bill Hickok.

I gasped. Then, without thinking, I asked out loud, "Where is the fucker?"

A male sounding voice answered. I didn't know then and I don't know now whether it was Marie using a low-pitched voice or Jon Luke speaking from Spookville. But I sure as shit know what that deep, chilling voice said.

Deadwood Gulch.

I began bawling like a God damned baby. The flame went out. Marie got up and re-lit the gaslamps on the wall. Then she came over to where I was sitting.

I stood up and she took me in her arms.

Our naked bodies were clasped together and I cried and I cried on her shoulder. She's so short I had to bend way over to do that, so she sat me back down on the chair, sat on my lap, let me empty every fucking tear I'd held back for the past ten years. I hadn't let myself cry since daddy'd died in my arms. I'd blubbered then, but not since, until now.

Now I knew for shit sure. Wild Bill's days were numbered. Somehow he knew that. Now I knew it too.

"You got anything to drink around here except that tea?" I asked her.

"Only a bottle of brandy," she said. "Do you drink brandy?"

"I sure as fuck do," I told her.

Over the next two hours, Marie and I killed a whole bottle of Californy brandy between the two of us.

.....

Well, it wasn't no surprise that Marie and I found ourselves together in her bed next, was it?

Now I want to tell you, Stranger. There ain't many things I like better in life than sucking cock. But there's times when there's absolutely nothing better than sucking a pair of gorgeous titties. And Marie's sweet little pointed tits with their rosebud nipples were 'bout as nice as anything I'd ever sucked. I sucked hers. She sucked mine. I fingered her cunt. She fingered mine. I took a swig of brandy. She took a swig. The saddest night I'd ever spent because of seeing that fucking bullet in the flame was made bearable by fucking and getting fucked by Madame Moustache.

She licked my body. What I mean to tell you is, there ain't an inch of skin on my body that didn't get tingled by Marie's skillful tongue. Yep, even my asshole if you have to know.

But when her lips and tongue got to my crack... Well, there ain't words to describe it.

I don't want you to get me wrong. I love to get done by men and boys. Always have. But there's one thing you fellows can never get right. You don't know how to work a clit. Certainly not with your clumsy fingers or your throbbing pricks. Not even with your tongues. Only a female can do it right.

Marie told me later that her cat Fifi can give great cunt-licks. Don't appeal to me none. Maybe you've gotta be French to want a cat to lick your twat.

But, forget about Fifi. Marie eats cunt as good a she sucks cock.

I've gotta admit, I gave her as good as I got. Except for licking her asshole. There ain't much where I draw the line. But that's just not something I do. Marie didn't seem to mind. Particularly when I got down to slobbering over her clit while I ran the fingers of one hand up her asshole while the fingers of my other hand gave her a fingerfuck that had her moaning like a sick mule.

I nuzzled my cheeks into that deep, soft bush of hers. I could have stayed there forever. I know I'll never find anyone else with as cozy a bush as the one Madame Moustache sports in that black triangle of hers.

. . . . .

It was nigh onto three in the morning when we'd killed the bottle and had come so often we were plumb worn out.

I asked Marie how much I owed her for the fuck.

"For a woman like you, I have a special rate," she answered.

"Yeah," I said. "I remember. Twenty dollars."

I reached into the pockets of my jeans that were still on the floor and fetched out the twenty dollar goldpiece I'd stashed away just for this. Marie was still in bed. She held out her hand. The coin disappeared into it.

She and I both knew I'd given as well as I'd got. But I understood that an arteest is an arteest. She's a professional. I'm an amateur.

Fair is fair, I always say.

. . . . .

So that was the night I cried over knowing for sure the bullet that had Wild Bill's name on it was right here in Deadwood Gulch. It was also the night I got one of my best fuckings ever.

And just thinking of that night can make me laugh and cry. And God almighty! I could sure use a drink. Well, thank you, Mister. You're a real gentleman.

. . . . .

I never told Wild Bill or Colorado Charlie about my see-ounce with Madame Moustache. I knew that Bill was right about never leaving Deadwood alive. I would just have to deal with it.

. . . . .

Charlie was ready to start his freight service. Bill had the financing figured out and Charlie had scouted out the routes he wanted to establish. All he needed now was the horses, the stage, and the drivers.

Him and me went down to Cheyenne to buy us some horses and a coach. We got us a fine team and a pretty fair coach. The coach needed some work done on it but Charlie can fix up just about anything you can think of. And I ain't half bad at that myself. By the time Charlie and me'd worked on the coach it was as good as any fucking vehicle in the West.

Charlie let it be known around Cheyenne that we were driving that stagecoach to Deadwood and before we left town we had passengers and freight to haul with us. Colorado Charlie never missed a chance to turn a dollar.

.....

When we drove that coach into Deadwood there was a cheering crowd there to greet us and our passengers. Colorado Charlie and Calamity Jane were real Deadwood celebrities. Shit, we still are. It seemed everybody in town wanted to welcome us back, us and our new stagecoach. Well, nearly everybody.

I suggested to Charlie that we stable the horses at Moccasin Varnes' place. His EQ Stables weren't the only ones in town. But I'd heard that Moccasin still had a kind of hardon for Wild Bill. He was grumbling around town that Bill was a cardshark and I was still in hopes that if we could get to be customers of his we could quiet him down.

I knew there wasn't much we could do to make friends with that fucking bastard Seth Bullock. But as far as I knew, the only thing Varnes had against Wild Bill was that he and his flunky Jack McCall had lost some money to him. My idea was that if we threw some business Varnes' way, he'd forget about losing at poker. Any gambler, except maybe Wild Bill or Madame Moustache, is bound to lose oncet in a while. Ain't that the fucking truth?

.....

Now that Colorado Charlie Utter's Freight and Passenger Service had horses and coach, it was necessary to hire some drivers.

Charlie is a naturally friendly man and most people like him. So he has a big circle of friends here in town. He also has fucked and been fucked by every pretty fairy miner in the Gulch. And not all those queer young miners had struck it rich in panning the creeks and streams of the Black Hills. A paying job looked mighty promising to a placer miner down on his luck.

From all the applicants, Charlie hired Handsome Harry Hawks as driver and Shorty McPhail as shotgun for the first trial run. Because it's one thing to be a good fuck and cocksucker and another to brave the roads and trails leading outta Deadwood, the jobs were understood to be temporary until the guys proved they were up to the task.

There was no freight or passenger service in place from Deadwood to Sundance at the time. And for a good reason. Sundance is a mining town that's a heap smaller than Deadwood. But at the time it was twice as lawless. And the Indians who lived in the hills along the dusty route were far from friendly. It took balls to get there. And even more balls to be in that town of thugs and desperados.

Charlie had already checked out Sundance, of course. Tough customers never fazed Charlie one bit. He'd run freight and passenger lines to the mining camps in Colorado and dealt with plenty of lawless types there. Later, him and Wild Bill had run a freight business together in Hays, Kansas. I can tell you from personal experience, that shithole crawls with every fucking slimebag you can imagine. So Charlie had no nevermind about scouting out Sundance as the first destination for the new business. He made four or five trips there, I don't remember which. And each time he came back to Deadwood he told me what he'd learned.

What it amounted to was this:

Dirty Dan Garrity and his Hole in the Wall Gang had been terrorizing all the Dakota Territory. It was Dirty Dan himself who found gold there in Sundance and settled his gang in town permanent.

When word got out there was gold in Sundance, there was a gold rush. But a very small fucking rush. To go pan gold in a town run by Dirty Dan Garrity and his Hole in the Wall Gang took more balls than what's possessed by your average cocksucker.

But lawless as the shithole was, Dirty Dan allowed people to run businesses there. And a hardware merchant by the name of Levi'd set up a store selling mining gear and equipment. He needed supplies from Deadwood, and was Charlie's first customer. So, the first run of the business was to haul picks and shovels and pans and boots and chamberpots to the miners in Sundance

. . . . .

Me and Wild Bill and Colorado Charlie were all down to the stagestop at the Palace Hotel on Sherman Street. It's still the stagestop. You probably got off the stage there yourself back when you came to Deadwood.

The stage was pretty well loaded up with miner hardware. There would've been room for a passenger. But what kinda crazy son of a bitch would wanna ride to a place as lawless as Sundance? As it turned out, no one.

We waved Handsome Harry and Shorty off and went across the street to the Gulch Saloon to wet our whistles.

Bill and Charlie and me stood at the bar just shooting the shit. Bill and Charlie were smoking and I was chawing and the booze they serve there ain't half bad. When the three of us got to working our jaws the time passed nice and sweet.

It wasn't much more than a couple of hours when there was a hullabaloo out on the street. Charlie went to the saloon door to take a gander and he came hustling back to the bar.

"C'mon, you two," he said. "It's our coach. It's already back."

"What the fuck?" Bill said. "What the shit-eating Hell's it doing back here in Deadwood?"

"We could stand here at the God damned bar all morning asking each other that same dumb-ass question," I said. "Or we could go out there and ask Handsome Harry and Shorty. It's just fucking possible one or t'other of 'em might have the answer."

That got us moving our asses out the door of the saloon and across the street to see what brought those two cocksuckers back to Deadwood instead of to Sundance where they were supposed to go.

When Handsome Harry and Shorty saw us, they hopped down from their seats.

Charlie saw one of his pretty boys among the crowd that'd gathered at the stage to see what all the fuss was about. Charlie paid the kid four bits to get up on the driver's seat and keep a watch on the team and the cargo. Bill was herding Handsome Harry and Shorty across the road to The Gulch to buy 'em a drink and find out what the fuck brought 'em back to Deadwood afore they delivered their cargo to Sundance.

It took two shots of rye whiskey for each of 'em afore Shorty could find the words to tell us what had happened.

"We was riding along smooth as birdshit," Shorty began. "Harry was making good time with the horses and I had all three of my God damned shotguns loaded and primed for action.

"We'd got on just fine and dandy for 'bout an hour or so. There's this place out there where the fucking trail makes a bend around a hill. You can't see around that curve for shit."

"I know the spot you're talking about there, Shorty," Colorado Charlie said.

That guy knows every inch of any trail oncet he's covered it himself. In his mind he was right there with Shorty while Shorty was spinning his yarn.

"We round that bend," Shorty continued, "and what do you think we seed?"

"Are we playing some kind of God damned guessing game here, Shorty?" I asked. "Get to the God damned fucking point, will you?"

"Yeah, sure, Calam," Shorty said. "What we seed was a band of Injuns."

"How big a band?" Wild Bill asked.

"'Bout five," Handsome Harry chimed in. The good-looking fairy finally got into the discussion. God, how I wished he wasn't queer. He's one sharp looking pilgrim. I'd love to suck whatever he has hanging behind his jeans. But, God damn it. I'm just not his type.

"Yeah," Shorty agreed. "'Bout five, maybe six. Injuns in feathers and warpaint. They didn't have no bows and arrows. But had army rifles instead."

"Were those five or six Injuns on horses or on foot?" Bill asked.

"Mounted," Handsome Harry said.

He was getting downright talkative. God, he's *so* fuckable.

"I hauled off and plugged the one in front," Shorty continued. "Shot him right off his God damned pony. That made the others hold back.

"Handsome Harry here, he got the fucking horses wheeled around back in this here direction and we high-tailed it back to Deadwood. The fucking Redskins didn't chase after us."

"And here we are," Handsome Harry said, not exactly adding

anything we couldn't see for ourselves.

"Is your bullwhip still there in the stage?" I asked Handsome Harry.

"Yeah, sure," he told me.

"And the shotguns, too?" Charlie asked Shorty.

"A course," Shorty replied.

Wild Bill set two bucks on the bar and told the barkeep to supply the boys with whiskey to sooth their nerves.

Wild Bill, Colorado Charlie, and me headed out the door for the coach. No one needed to say nothing. We all knew exactly what we had to do.

Charlie told the fairy to get down off the driver's seat. I took that seat and picked up the blacksnake. Charlie got up there beside me and grabbed a shotgun. We checked to make sure there was a few extra loaded shotguns under the seat ready to take care of as many as five intruders. Wild Bill got in the coach in the passenger's seat.

We headed back outta town. We was going to make our delivery to Sundance. And we all three hoped to Hell to meet those fucking Injuns along the way and take care of a little problem that'd crept up on the trail.

You wouldn't happen to wanna buy a lady a little snort, would you, Mister? You would? Well bless your fucking heart. Thank you.

.....

We hauled ass down the dirt road keeping a keen watch out for any sign of movement anywhere. After about an hour Colorado Charlie gave me a nudge.

"It's right around that curve ahead that Handsome Harry and Shorty ran into them Redskins."

He had his shotgun in readiness for trouble.

And sure enough, right around that bend there was trouble enough waiting for us. Five mounted sons of bitches in headdresses and warpaint, armed with rifles, popped outta the trees.

The one in front fired on us. At that close distance the asshole missed us by a mile. Couldn't shoot for shit. I flicked my bullwhip at the son of a bitch and hit him square between the eyes. The bastard fell off his pony and went screaming and writhing into the dust.

The other four must of decided they didn't want any of that

shit and tried to turn tail. Before they'd even swung around, Wild Bill jumped from down inside the coach, got one in the head, and Colorado Charlie put a hole through another with his shotgun.

Just then, thundering down the hill on a white stallion came a masked white man with a drawn pistol. Would you believe it? It was Deadwood Dick, in person. Charlie'd picked up the second shotgun to shoot the intruder. I knocked the gun aside as I pulled the coach to a halt.

The fifth war-painted cocksucker got away. Shit!

The stranger on the white horse dismounted next to the asshole I'd stung with my blacksnake. The bastard was wriggling and screaming something awful.

Bill and Charlie and me got down and out of the coach and approached the masked man and the squirmer.

"Wild Bill and Colorado Charlie," I said. "I'd like you to meet my good friend, Deadwood Dick."

Of course, they'd already met my sweetie before, when he'd appeared on the scene back there by Four Corners, but no one said anything about having met before.

The three guys shook hands all around while we all kept an eye on the bawling human mess who was squawking at our feet.

"Hell," Charlie said, taking a close gander at the yipping son of a bitch. "That cocksucker ain't no Injun. He's a Celestial."

Charlie's an expert on a passel of things. And Injuns is one of 'em. He's lived among a bunch of tribes, has slept with 'em, eaten with 'em, and fucked 'em. He can speak about a dozen of their languages. If Charlie says the cocksucker at our feet ain't no Injun, he ain't no Injun. Case closed.

"Now what would a bunch of Celestials wanna put on headdresses and warpaint and come out here to interrupt your stage for?" Deadwood Dick asked.

"We'll find out for ourselves real soon," Wild Bill said.

He reached down, grabbed the Celestial by his pigtail and lifted him up by his hair.

The Celestial began to scream bloody murder.

Bill shook the shit outta him.

"Shut up, you fucker," he growled.

Every time the Celestial let out a scream he got a new shaking up. He got the idea pretty soon and shut his God damned trap.

"Who are you?" Bill asked.

"Hu Yu," his victim answered.

That pissed Bill off royally.

He kept shaking the fellow and kept getting the same dumbshit answer.

Finally Charlie got the picture.

"Knock it off, Bill," he said. "The fucker's name is Hu Yu. That ain't what we need to know. What we gotta find out is who set this bunch of Celestials on the trail to fuck up our freight business. Give the cocksucker to me."

Bill lifted Hu Yu by the hair and passed him over to Charlie.

Deadwood Dick was laughing his ass off, he thought it was so God damned funny. I sidled up to my boyfriend and asked him what he was doing out here.

"I didn't know the stagecoach was yourn," he said. "I was just a-doing some road agenting to pick me up some loot to give to the poor. Glad I was here, though. I've missed you something awful, Calam."

"Me, too," I confessed.

"Where you heading?" he asked.

"Sundance," I told him.

"Meet me there," he said, and rode off.

Bill and Charlie didn't give a shit about Deadwood Dick and didn't pay no nevermind to his leaving. They were plenty interested in Hu Yu, though.

Charlie held his bowie knife at Hu's throat.

"Who set you up to this?" he asked. "Tom Ng?"

The mention of Tom Ng sent Hu into a shrieking fit.

"Tom Ng kill me. Better you kill me, Mister," he screamed.

Colorado Charlie let loose of the bastard.

"Reckon we've got our answer," he said. "Tom Ng dressed these Celestials up as Injuns and set 'em against our stage. And we know who's in cahoots with Tom Ng."

"That son of a bitching bastard Seth Bullock," I spit.

"Right," Bill said. "Not much we can do 'bout it. Can't prove nothing. But there's no question now 'bout who's our God damned enemy. We watch our asses double-time from now on."

"What we going to do about Hu?" I asked.

"Leave the cocksucker out here to fend for himself. He won't dare go back to Deadwood and get himself tortured by Tom Ng for fucking up. He might make it to Sundance or get caught by real Injuns. Who gives a shit? C'mon. We've got a delivery to make to Sundance."

So we went back to our stage and headed down the road to Sundance, leaving Hu Yu blubbering by the side of the trail.

.....

The rest of our drive to Sundance was dusty but uneventful. The end of the line was at Poker Pete's Saloon, the biggest building in Sundance.

We got down right in front of the saloon and tethered the team. Bill had his two Colts in his sash like always. Charlie had his fully loaded shotgun. And I kept my bullwhip with me.

There weren't many folks in the one street in town. But when we entered the saloon it was filled with as filthy and slimy a bunch of ruffians as I've seen anywhere in my life. And let me tell you, Pilgrim. I've seen and lived among the dregs of the West in my time.

When the three of us stepped in the door, all fifty or sixty desperados shut the fuck up and stared at us. There was a lady singer up on the stage and a piany player and damned if they didn't stop in mid-note to stare along with the scumbags.

A particularly rotten looking bag of shit came ambling up to Colorado Charlie and shook his hand. Turned out he was Dirty Dan himself, the leader of the Hole in the Wall Gang.

"Glad you made it with our supplies, Pardner," he said. "Levi the storekeeper was about out of thundermugs. Another day gone by and most of the town'd be shitting in the street."

Charlie introduced us.

"The three of you step up to the bar," Dirty Dan said. "The drinks are on the house for you three."

That was a very nice thing for Dirty Dan to say. And the very last decent thing I ever did hear him say.

The canary up on the stage got to warbling again and the dude on the music box took time off from scratching his balls to accompany her. The barkeep, Poker Pete, sneered at us and served us something between mule piss and swamp water. Not that we didn't down the stuff. A drink's a drink, I always say.

When Wild Bill and Colorado Charlie'd downed their shots and hove up to leave I told 'em, "Boys. I reckon I'll stay here a mite. When your next coach pulls into Sundance, I'll catch it back to Deadwood."

That didn't seem to surprise Bill or Charlie none. Hardly nothing does. Same as if one of 'em had told me he was going to do a wardance on Main Street. Shit! I wouldn't bat an eye, either. No one of the three of us told no one else what the fuck to do or not to do. That's why we all got along so good.

I went to the saloon door and waved them adios. Then I went back into Poker Pete's to wait for my boyfriend Deadwood Dick to get to Sundance.

.....

I was ambling back to the bar to get me another shot of Poker Pete's mule piss to keep me company while I waited for Deadwood Dick to get his ass to Sundance. I was working my way through that dense pack of ruffians when I feel some cocksucker grab my wrist.

"Where the fuck do you think *you're* going?"

The gruff voice belonged to none other than Dirty Dan. And the tone was anything but friendly.

"Take your shit-eating hands off me, Asshole," I growled.

That got me a fist in the chops. Dirty Dan didn't have very good manners.

"Take that, you fucking bitch," he said. "I run this town. I run this saloon. I run this gang. And I'll be hornswaggled if I don't run all the gals in this town. Of which there are exactly two...you and Virgie Beaubeaux."

I swore on the spot that I would clean that cocksucker's clock afore the day was over.

I did me some fast arithmetic and came to the conclusion that Virgie Beaubeaux had to be the canary up on the stage singing *There'll be a hot time in the old town tonight.*

"We ain't got no whores here in town yet," Dirty Dan continued. "On account of I ain't been able to find no cocksucking whoremaster yet wants to haul his girls to this shithole of a town.

"So here's where you come in, you fucking bitch. You can get your ass up them stairs to the upstairs rooms we built for the whores whenever they get here. Take off those duds and be the first pussy for sale in town. Or you can get the fuck up there on the stage with Miss Virgie and entertain me and the boys with some snappy songs and patter. But you don't just loll around here like some kind of God damned decoration. Get it?"

I got it. I could tell that if I didn't play his little game, there'd probably be a gang rape right there in Poker Pete's Saloon. And I knew who'd be at the bottom of that pile of filthy drunks.

"I'll entertain your boys with the most entertaining shit that's ever hit this shithole," I told him.

So up onto the stage I climbed.

. . . . .

I've entertained the boys at most of the theater saloons west of the Kansas-Missouri line. And, if I do say so myself, I'm damned entertaining.

Here in Deadwood old Al Swearengen calls on me 'bout oncet a month to put on an act at his Gem Theater. Get on over there next time I'm doing my damned act. You'll get a big kick outta it.

Miss Virgie was surprised as Hell to see me get up on the stage with her. The piany player wasn't impressed one way or t'other. He was too busy trying to itch away the cooties that musta been playing cowboys and Injuns on his balls.

"Can you sing *Oh, Susanna?*" I asked Miss Virgie.

She smiled at me real pretty.

"Sure can, Lady," she said.

"Call me Calam," I asked her.

"Nice to meet you, Calam," she said. "I'm Virgie Beaubeaux. And that over there on the piany. That's Gloomy Gus."

"We're gonna make beautiful music together, Miss Virgie," I said.

I walked over to Gloomy Gus.

"Howdy, Gus," I said. "Miss Virgie and me is gonna do a duet. How 'bout you step aside here for a moment, and you can scratch your balls in that there corner."

Gloomy Gus didn't change expression and didn't remove his hand from his crotch. He just got up from his chair at the piany and went over to the side of the stage.

"Okey, doke," I said to Miss Virgie. "Let's give the boys a fucking earful of *Oh, Susanna.*"

I stood myself 'bout fifteen foot away from the piany with my blacksnake in hand. Miss Virgie stood next to me facing the shitty bastards in the audience.

I flicked my bullwhip at the piany, hitting one ivory at a time, accompanying Miss Virgie. Like to brought the house down. It wows 'em every time.

When Miss Virgie'd sung all seven verses of *Susanna* she asked me if I knew any other piece I could play on the piany with my blacksnake.

"I only know two God damn pieces," I told her. "*Susanna* and *Clementine*. Do you know Clementine?"

"You bet your sweet ass I do," she told me.

"How many verses?" I asked.

"All twenty-five," she said.

Jesus Christ! Nearly every canary on the stages in the West has to sing *Clementine* at least oncet on every stage. But I'd never heard of no one do more'n 'bout eleven or twelve verses. I knew that if we could give the assholes twenty-five verses they'd be eating right outta our fucking hands.

I stepped back 'bout three more paces. Truth is it's just as easy to hit the keys farther back like that as closer. But it makes it look harder. Any bullwhackers in the audience would know that. But decent bullwhackers are as rare as a turd without flies.

Miss Virgie and me gave 'em twenty-five verses of Clementine, each one raunchier than the one before. There wasn't a hole in Clementine's body didn't get fucked, sucked, fingered, and rammed by miners, donkeys, mules, deacons, squirrels, and paper collars. I'd never heard the like and neither had the cocksuckers in the hall. They was laughing and hooting and hollering and falling all over the God damned floor. Even those two shitheels, Dirty Dan and Poker Pete was having themselves a time. The only one not laughing was Gloomy Gus. I guess he was too wrapped in trying to relieve his itches to pay much attention to the act Miss Virgie and me were putting on.

When we was through with that act, I asked the audience, "Send me up a spittoon."

A big moose of a guy picked up a brass spittoon and hurled it up at me. I caught it easy.

I set the God damned spittoon six feet away and took a chaw of 'baccy.

"Any of you fuckers wanna bet me four bits I can't hit the spittoon dead on at this distance?"

The Moose shouted, "Four bits says you cain't."

"You're on," I said.

I noticed a bunch of the boys were taking bets from each other. Some betting I could do it, some that I couldn't.

Ptui! I landed a gob right in the hole. The Moose tossed four bits onto the stage. Miss Virgie picked up the coins for me.

"Double the distance for me, Miss Virgie," I asked.

She hauled it the distance I asked.

"Any son of a bitch out there man enough to bet I can't hit the fucker at that distance?"

The Moose shouted, "I'll risk four bits just to see you try, Lady."

The room buzzed with suckers betting each other that I could or couldn't make it.

Ptui! Right into the God damned opening.

This time not only Moose's four bits, but a bunch of other coins came clattering onto the stage. I had those sons of bitches purring like baby kittens.

"Okay, boys," I said. "Now I'll tell you 'bout the time I fucked Jesse James while diddling his God damned brother."

Did I ever tell you that story? It's one of my regular ones down to the Gem Theater. No? Come on down sometime. It's a dandy. Do you happen to have a quarter to buy a lady a drink? Thank you, Pard. I won't forget you.

.....

"C'mon, Lady," Moose yelled. "Tell us later. Have Miss Virgie move the fucking spittoon another three foot away. Give me a chance to win back my money. A whole buck says you cain't do it."

I'd done my 'baccy spitting act maybe 'bout a hundred times afore. And there was always someone in the crowd wanted me to have a go at it a third time.

"What d'you all say, Boys?" I asked. "Should I give the gentleman a chance to recoup his losses?"

Of course pandemonium broke loose. Every God damned shit eating bastard wanted me to try. I knew not one of 'em could hit a spittoon at the new distance. They wanted to see if I could do it.

The betting out there was fast and furious.

I took me a new chaw and built up a gob the size of a goat turd.

Ptui!
What do you think, Pilgrims? Did I hit the fucking spittoon?
I've never missed a shot like that in my life.
The place went crazy

.....

I had to keep the galoots entertained 'til Deadwood Dick got there. I thought I'd keep my Jesse James story available for later. So I began to recite some of my poems for 'em.

Whenever a bunch of us bullwhackers come to camp at the end of the day around the campfire, we always tell tall tales or take turns telling limericks. From listening and remembering them poems, I've memorized over a hundred. So I began to give them bastards one after another, knowing I could keep it going until my masked boyfriend walked through the saloon door.

There oncet was hermit named Dave,
Who kept a dead whore in his cave.
He said, "I'll admit
I'm a bit of a shit.
But think of the money I save."

You might wonder why I chose that one for beginners. Easy. Dirty Dan'd told me there warn't no whoremaster in camp. That meant that the only men in town who were getting any were the queers. The straight guys had to be content with fucking their fist. Fucking a dead whore would seem pretty funny to them. And, as it turned out, they liked that one a lot.

You've probably heard it afore. That's 'cause I made it famous there in Sundance and it's been told on every stage since then. It got the audience warmed up for my poetry reading.

I knew one about a barkeep named Poker Pete. And since there was a Poker Pete who was a barkeep in this shithole, I socked that one to 'em.

There oncet as a barkeep named Pete
Who was really a bit indiscreet.
He pulled on his dong

'Til it grew really long
And it actually dragged in the street.

The boys really liked that one, and it even made Poker Pete laugh his ass off. I was still warming up the house.

I was beginning to wonder when Deadwood Dick would arrive on the scene. My throat was getting bone dry telling my poems. But I managed to start a new one anyway, hoping it might bring in my boyfriend.

"Here's one you galoots might like," I said. "It's about a famous bandit like you-all are. But he also happens to be my lover. Would you like to hear it?"

I got a big, resounding cheer in response.

"Okay, then, Boys. Here it goes:

A fellow from Deadwood named Dick
Liked to feel my hot hand on his prick.
He taught me to fool
With his rigid straight tool
'Til the cream shot out, warm, white, and thick.

At that very moment, the saloon door swung in and who do you suppose stepped in, pistol drawn and mask in place?

You guessed it. My lover, Deadwood Dick.

Dirty Dan swung around, drawing his pistol.

I knew Deadwood Dick never kept no bullets in his gun. I was afraid maybe he'd be a goner.

Right behind Deadwood Dick, a second person came bursting in. A little guy in warpaint.

"Hu Yu!" I cried out.

"Who's who?" Dirty Dan asked, confused.

I flicked my blacksnake out from the stage and hit Dirty Dan on the hand. That made him drop his gun as he shook his fist and danced up and down in pain.

Deadwood Dick, quick as a wink, scooped up the fallen pistol and threw it directly up on the stage to me.

I took deadly aim at my enemy and shot point blank.

I got that son of a bitching cocksucker Dirty Dan dead to rights. Right in the fucking heart. He sprawled out on the floor, blood spurting all over the God damned place. It was a sight for sore eyes.

Hu Yu took one look at the gore and turned tail. It'd taken him a long time to get to the God damned saloon. But he was outta there lickety-split.

That bunch of evil cocksuckers looked bug-eyed at their leader, dead as donkey shit on the floor of that saloon. Then they looked up slack-jawed at me on the stage. They didn't know whether to shit or go blind.

"Remove your mask," I ordered Dick.

Deadwood Dick knew that the moment had come for him to assume a new character. He whipped off that mask and threw it onto the floor.

I tossed the pistol back to him and he caught it by the handle and pointed it all around the room.

"Look at him, boys," I shouted out. "There's your new leader, the Sundance Kid."

I flicked my blacksnake across the stage.

"Anyone who don't accept Sundance as your leader, speak up now. Then you can feel the kiss of my blacksnake."

Not a one of them sons of bitches stirred.

Sundance," I said to my boyfriend. "Deadwood Dick's days with his empty gun are over. Keep your pistol loaded and your eyes open from now on. Meet the Hole in the Wall Gang…your very own gang, now.

"Any one of you galoots who'd care to piss on Dirty Dan can do so now," I told the gang members. "Anyone who pisses on him gets a free drink at the bar courtesy of Calamity Jane."

You know what? I bought forty drinks of Poker Pete's whiskey for the boys that afternoon.

By the way. The rye they serve in this here joint beats the Hell outta Poker Jack's mule piss. Why, don't mind if I do, Stranger. You're quite a doll. Thank you.

.....

Sundance and Miss Virgie and me took ourselves up the stairs to one of them rooms they had there. Gloomy Gus stayed up on the stage tinkling the keys while the Gang was whooping it up something fierce.

Me and Sundance and Miss Virgie shed our clothes fast as

dripping snot. Miss Virgie was a sight to behold. Greatest set of knockers I'd laid eyes on for weeks. And Sundance! This was the first time I'd seen him completely naked. That is, without his God damned mask on. And I'm telling you, Pilgrim. There ain't a handsomer face in the West.

But his best feature ain't his face. That pecker of his is so fuckable and suckable that I couldn't waste too much time admiring that unmasked face.

And didn't the three of have ourselves a time! I got fucked by Sundance while I was sucking Miss Virgie's luscious titties at the same time. Then I was eating Miss Virgie's cunt while she was sucking Sundance's cock. Then...Oh, Hell! I could spend the whole rest of the evening telling you 'bout the time the three of us had. But I got to go to the pisspot and pee.

If you wanna hang around 'til I get back, I'll tell you 'bout the worst day that ever dawned in the West.

That day was August two, 1876. If you're not up to a tear-jerking tale, you'd best not be at this here bar when I get back. Cause I'm feeling myself in the mood to tell you 'bout that motherfucking day.

Chapter Four

THE DEATH OF THE WILD WEST

Howdy, folks. I'm back. Well lookie here. A bigger crowd at the bar than when I left. What did you folks all expect from me? My story 'bout how I fucked Jesse James that time while I was jacking off his brother Frank at the same time? Sorry. If that's what you're here for, you might as well vamoose right now. I'm a-going to tell that yarn at the Gem down the street next Friday night. Up on the stage. I'll throw in some rope tricks, too. And maybe recite some of the limericks I picked up from my bullwhacking days.

No, what I'm in the mood to tell you 'bout now is how that motherfucking little cocksucker Jack McCall shot and killed the last great gunslinger in the West. On that day, it wasn't only my husband, Wild Bill Hickok, who died. On that day, the Wild West itself died.

Things've never been the same since. An era died. And from that era only two of the old-timers have survived. Me and Colorado Charlie Utter.

Some of you know that Wild Bill and me had an inkling his time was 'bout up. We didn't know what day it was gonna happen. But we knew that day was not far off.

. . . . .

There generally ain't too much to do here in Deadwood in the mornings. So we tend to stay up late at night a-hooting and a-hollering. Then most folks sleep it off 'til 'bout noon the next day. You know how it is.

On that August morning, Bill and Charlie and me slept in at our rooms at the Overland 'til maybe ten, ten-thirty. Bill and Charlie hied themselves off to the bathhouse while I stayed in the hotel room sponging myself off and stuff.

When the boys got back all squeaky clean, the three of us went across the street to the Conestoga Saloon for what Wild Bill called our morning cocktail. That's the name he'd picked up in the East for a shot of rye. Bill loves fancy words.

By the time we'd downed one, two, or three cocktails it was time for lunch.

Sometimes time sure flies, don't it?

We walked ourselves down to the Eatephone at 109 Main Street where Wong Chong dishes out better than average grub. Go on over there if you wanna buy yourself some good eating. What we had was generous servings of pot roast, potatoes, peas and carrots, cherry pie, and coffee. There's not much about that day I don't 'member down to every fucking little detail.

After we'd stuffed our faces, Bill was hankering to play himself some poker. He told us he was heading for Nuttall and Mann's No. 10. He'd been playing cards there the night afore with Carl Mann, Charlie Rich, and Cap'n Massie. He'd told 'em he'd be back to continue the friendly game that morning.

Colorado Charlie had his own plans for what he had to do after lunch. His new pony express business between Deadwood and Fort Laramie'd only been operating for four days. But it was already a success. He headed for the Palace Hotel which was where he'd set up his headquarters for the pony express as well as his passenger and freight service.

Me? I went to wet my whistle and gab with the barflies at the Little Bonanza Saloon. I wanted to down a few pick-me-ups afore heading to the No. 10 where I might be able to make myself useful signaling to Wild Bill any information I could gather 'bout what the fellers he was playing with had in their hands.

So, after I'd had a drink or two at the Little Bonanza and I'd entertained the folks there with a few yarns, I left for where Bill was gambling.

I was armed with my blacksnake and my Colt. With Wild Bill's presentiment of death, and the vision I'd had of the engraved bullet at Madame Moustache's, I was never without my gun and whip in the streets of Deadwood.

.....

I'd got down the street just past the Banner Grocery Store when I spotted a figure bursting outta the No. 10. It was a kinda skinny hombre dressed in black. That was all I could tell right then. A brown horse was tethered to the railing outside the saloon. The guy puts his foot in the stirrup, bolts up onto the saddle, and what d'you know? The God damned saddle flips round to the horse's belly. Lands the asshole plop into the mud and shit. It was clear the saddle'd been slacked because it was a powerful hot day.

Now I recognized who the fucker was, even though he was covered all over with horseshit and mud. It was Jack McCall.

Jack struggles back up to his feet, looks around desperately, and takes off running down the street. He had a pistol in his hand and dropped it in the road.

I could see where the bastard was running to. It was toward the EQ Stables where he had a job shoveling shit.

Three fellers burst outta the No. 10 shouting and pointing.

"Wild Bill's been shot." "Murder!" "Catch the son of a bitch."

Talk about stunned. Wild Bill shot. Murdered. Murdered by that tiny pricked motherfucker Jack McCall.

What I wanted to do was go into the No. 10 to tend to my husband, Wild Bill. But that's not what my feet wanted to do. Them feet took off after the cocksucker who'd pulled the trigger on Bill.

McCall ran into the stable. I was a faster runner than him and had 'bout caught up with him.

I get inside the stable and the no good motherfucker wasn't much more than twenty feet away, hauling ass as fast as his little legs'd go.

I whip out the blacksnake and it catches him square on the ass. Knocks the son of a bitch flat on the stable floor, howling and screaming like a stuck pig.

He was a-screaming there inside the stable. I could hear there was a crowd gathering outside. I knew no one was like to enter 'cause I guess I was the only one knowed McCall was no longer armed.

I stood over the squirming weasel.

"Shut up, McCall, you fucking asshole," I told him, my pistol aimed right at his head.

He quieted right down, but he was still hurting real bad from his stinging butt.

"Listen to me real good, you prick," I continued. "You got a fast choice to make. You take too long to decide, you're dog food. Got it?"

He nodded his head.

"I want you to tell me who set you up to kill Wild Bill. You're too fucking stupid to do it all by yourself. If you keep your trap shut and don't tell me, I'm gonna shoot you slow, real slow."

I stepped back about ten paces.

"First I'll shoot this foot."

I took a shot that barely grazed his left foot. The bastard yipped something fierce.

"Then I'll put a hole through this one."

And I shot a bullet so close to his right foot I thought he'd pee his pants.

When the crowd outside heard the two shots they grew real quiet. 'Cause they couldn't figure out what was going on inside. But it was clear someone had a gun and no one wanted to come in while there was shooting going on.

"Next thing," I told the little creep, "I'll put a bullet through each of your hands. And if you haven't told me by then who set you up, I'll shoot off that tiny cock and those midget balls of yourn."

I let go a whip with the blacksnake and caught him square on the crotch. You've never heard such bawling in your life. I sure caught the cocksucker's attention.

"Now listen up," I continued. "If you tell me, right now, who's in this with you, all I'll do is turn you over to the crowd outside. No matter what they do to you, it won't be half as bad as what I'm 'bout to do."

"Don't shoot me, Calam," he said, rubbing his crotch real tender like. The man was in severe pain. "For God's sake don't shoot me to pieces. It's Varnes."

"Your boss, Moccasin Varnes?" I asked.

"Yeah. Moccasin paid me to do it. I didn't want to kill Wild Bill. But I sure needed the dough."

"How much did he pay you?" I asked.

"Twenty dollars," he said. "That's a powerful lot of money, Calam," he whimpered. "And I was in deep debt to Moccasin."

I've never been so pissed off at no one in my life. Jesus Christ! Twenty dollars to kill the greatest man who walked the trails of the West.

I spit on Jack's face and went to the stable doors.

"C'mon in, Boys," I shouted to the crowd. "The rotten little bastard's in here holding onto his balls and waiting for you to string him up."

I stepped back to let 'em in.

And, Jesus fucking Christ! Who's the first galoot through the door? I'll be fucked if it wasn't that son of a bitch Seth Bullock. And right behind him? Fucking Johnnie Moccasin Varnes.

Behind those two motherfuckers was a crowd of 'bout twenty pilgrims.

I was flabbergasted. Not a fucking thing I could do 'bout it.

Seth stepped up to Jack McCall who was more concerned 'bout his stinging peter than 'bout anything else at the moment.

"Jack McCall," Bullock said. "As sheriff of this here town I arrest you for the murder of Wild Bill Hickok."

That surprised the Hell outta me.

"Get this man up on his feet," Seth ordered. "He's gotta stand trial."

Three of the men in the crowd pulled Jack up onto his feet.

"We're gonna administer frontier justice," Seth said. "We're holding a fair trial across the street at McDaniel's Theater. Take the prisoner over there and I'll set up the machinery for the proceedings soon's we all get ourselves quieted down and thinking straight."

They hauled Jack McCall outta there and hustled him across the road to the theater.

I wanted to go tend to Wild Bill. When I got to the No. 10, Colorado Charlie was already there, tears running down his cheeks. I hadn't had time to cry 'til then myself.

There was Wild Bill's body, stretched out on the saloon floor. The barkeep, Harry Young, who'd known Wild Bill from clear back in the Hays days, had pulled a tablecloth over Bill's body, except for his head.

Harry's face was as tear-stained as mine and Charlie's.

"I've sent for Doc McDougal, Reverend Smith, and Digger Dixon," Harry said. "Them three'll take care of the burial details. Don't you worry none. Wild Bill will be treated with dignity. I'll see to that."

"What now?" Colorado Charlie said.

I told him there was a trial a-brewing at McDaniel's Theater for Jack McCall. We needed to get there pronto to see the little fucker get tried and hung.

We left Wild Bill's body with Harry and got our asses over to the theater. I explained everything I knew to Charlie on the way.

.....

When we got to the theater the house was packed. Everyone in Deadwood, it seemed, wanted to see the trial of the man who had killed Wild Bill Hickok. Charlie and me stood at the side by the door. I couldn't have sat still for the life of me. Neither could Charlie. Wild Bill's body was laying back there where we'd left it on the floor of the saloon, watched over by Harry Young. By now the doc, the preacher and the undertaker would be there. Them three always had plenty of work on their hands taking care of the remains of the men murdered real regular like here in town. It was Wild Bill's turn to be their customer now. And me and Charlie figured Jack McCall would be their next customer.

Up on the stage that bastard Seth Bullock was strutting around like Chief Big Shit. Jack McCall was sitting in a chair and had two big husky miners on each side of him to keep him from bolting. There was a kind of stand set up in front of the stage.

Seth Bullock stepped up to that there stand and everyone shut their traps to hear what he was gonna say.

"Citizens of Deadwood," Bullock began. "A man has been shot and killed in our town today. A notable citizen known to us as Wild Bill Hickok. His alleged murderer, Jack McCall, the accused, sits here on this stage facing you and facing the justice of his peers.

"As sheriff of this town, I hereby declare this theater a court of law to try the defendant. In my capacity as the only lawman around, I appoint Johnnie Varnes judge of this court."

I like to shit. Varnes was guiltier than McCall. I thought Charlie might throw a rampage. We could both see the way the wind was blowing. But we bided our time. No matter how this so-called trial went, we knew Jack McCall and Moccasin Varnes had already been tried by a jury of the two of us. And them two sons of bitches, Moccasin Varnes and Jack McCall would pay. No one fucks with Calamity Jane or anything that's hers without getting fucked over three times as bad. And I knew Colorado Charlie always evened up his scores too.

Moccasin came up to that stand and shook Fucking-bastard Bullock's hand.

"Mister Sheriff," he said. "I am proud of this honor you have bestowed on me. Though Deadwood is not governed by the laws of the United States of America as yet, I declare that we are not a barbarous city. The fate of the accused will be determined in a right legal manner just as if we was in Cheyenne or Washington. We'll have ourselves a trial by jury, by God."

Everyone but me and Charlie clapped and hooted and hollered at that.

"First off," Varnes continued. "I'm going to appoint me a jury. As I name the members of this here jury, I want 'em each to come up here to the front and stand facing you all."

Again, hooting and hollering in approval.

Judge Johnnie Moccasin Varner then named twelve of the God damnedest, filthiest, least law abiding sons of bitches who ever fucked up the Black Hills. They was all his own men. Me and Charlie knew this court would let Jack McCall off. But we also knew he'd face a higher court afterwards. The court of Calamity Jane and Colorado Charlie.

As Varnes called out the names of his chosen henchmen, each one came lumbering up front to the stupid applause and shouts of the audience. The twelve of 'em stood grinning at us in the audience.

Then he said, real solemn like:

"Since we ain't got enough chairs up here on this stage to seat these upstanding members of the jury, I'm going to ask 'em to go back to their seats and listen attentively to the evidence as it gets presented."

The twelve scoundrels returned to their seats and the so-called trial began.

Varnes cleared his throat.

"Jack," he said to McCall. "Stand up!"

McCall rose.

"You've heard the accusation, Jack. You have been accused of murdering Wild Bill Hickok. How do you plead? Guilty or not guilty?"

Jack replied, "I ain't guilty of nothing, Moccasin. And you know it."

"Sit down, Jack," Varnes said.

"Now, what we need here is a witness for the God damned prosecution. Anyone here have anything to say?"

Charlie Rich, one of the gamblers Wild Bill often played with stood up.

"Yeah, Moccasin," he shouted. "I'd like to tell everybody what happened back there at the Number Ten."

"Come on up here to the stage and say your piece, Charlie," Varnes invited.

Charlie Rich left his seat and went up on the stage. He stood at the stand and spoke out.

"Well, here's the way it was, Folks. I was sitting at the Number Ten playing a friendly game of poker with Wild Bill, Cap'n Massie, and Carl Mann. Usually Wild Bill sits with his back to the wall on account of he was a gunslinger and never knowed when some son of a bitch was gonna come after him. Except this time. Wild Bill arrived after we all was seated and Carl was in the corner seat. Well, sir. for one reason or t'other Bill decided not to make an issue of it, and took a chair that left his back sides open to the bar.

"We played a couple of hands, and Cap'n Massie was having himself a kind of a run of luck. As a matter of fact, Wild Bill, he said something like 'Looks like Lady Luck's sitting in your lap, Cap'n.' Something like that. I don't remember exactly.

"Next thing you know, I hear a shot. We all look up and see that son of a bitch Jack McCall with a pistol in his hand. The bastard is saying, 'Take that, you son of a bitch.' The dirty little coward shot Wild Bill in the back. Then the asshole goes running out the door and poor Wild Bill slumps over the table, his cards still in his hand. You could see right away he was dead as cowshit. And it was that fucking little coward sitting in that chair over there who shot the best man I ever knew in the back. If anyone should be strung up on that tree out there, it's Jack McCall."

There was a sprinkling of applause from the audience. But most everyone was kinda quiet and thinking 'bout that scene at the No. 10 they'd just heard.

Varnes came back up to the stand. He addressed Jack.

"Okay, Jack," he said. "You've heard the prosecution. What do you have to say for yourself? Address the jury out there."

Jack McCall stood up and kinda strutted to the stand. You could tell he wasn't afraid. He knew he'd get off Scot free, and showed it.

"I'll tell you how it was, Moccasin," he began.

"Don't tell me, Jack. Tell the jury out there," Varnes ordered.

"All right, Moccasin" McCall agreed. "Well, men. I have but few words to say. Wild Bill killed my brother and I killed him. Wild Bill threatened to kill me if I crossed his path. I ain't sorry for what I done. And I'd do the same thing all over again."

Varnes told Jack to go back to his chair and sit down.

That's what the li'l fucker did.

Charlie and me knew Jack's story was a crock of shit. But what could we do?

Charlie whispered to me. "I know Wild Bill didn't have nothing to do with McCall's fucking brother. I'm gonna find out if he's even got a brother. And if he does, we'll take it from there."

Varnes was speaking to his audience now.

"All right, everyone. We've heard the evidence. The jury's gonna stay here at McDaniel's and the rest of us is going to the scene of the alleged crime. When the jury has reached a verdict, they'll bring it to the Number Ten. For now, though, let's all of us clear the Hell outta here and see how the whiskey is at the Number Ten. The sheriff will see that the accused is brought to the saloon, won't you Seth?"

Bullock said he'd see to it.

.....

Charlie and me was the last ones outta the theater, and the last ones to get to the place where Wild Bill was shot. When we got there, the doc, the digger and the preacher'd done whatever had to be done to get Bill's body removed. And Harry'd got the blood all mopped up.

Of course, the No. 10 was packed. Me and Charlie had ourselves a Hell of a time even getting up to the bar. The owner, Bill Nuttall, was tending bar. I asked him where Harry was.

"Harry and Carl are over to the undertaker's, Calam. They want you to know everything's being taken care of real respectful."

Bill slipped me and Charlie a couple of drinks on the house. That helped some.

Finally, 'bout a half-hour later, Seth Bullock barges into the saloon. Everyone shut up real fast to see what he had to say.

Of course, Moccasin was already at the No. 10 and he walked through the crowd to where Seth was.

Seth opened his fucking yap to speak. He shouted out the door.

"Carl and Sammie. Bring in the accused to hear the sentence."

The two bruisers came through the door with Jack McCall between 'em. Jack was looking right smug.

"Judge Varnes," Seth said. "The jury is prepared to render its verdict."

The twelve jurymen managed to squeeze into the crowded room. They just barely got all twelve of their asses in. Charlie Whitehead was the foreman and he was beaming something fierce.

"Charlie," Varnes said. "What is the verdict of the jury?"

"Your Honor," Whitehead announced. "We the members of the jury unanimously find Jack McCall not guilty by reason of self-defense and the biblical rule of an eye for an eye. Wild Bill killed Jack's brother. The jury considers his revenge justified."

Well, Sir. More fights broke out in that saloon than I'd ever seed at any one time at any one place. Charlie and me knowed what the rigged jury would decide. It surprised 'bout half the folks there in the saloon, though.

It was Varnes' turn to do his part. But it was too noisy for anyone to hear him declare that Shit-ass Jack McCall was free.

Carl and Sammie got Jack out the door fast. Charlie and me tried to get out right behind him, but Seth Bullock stood in our way with his six-shooter drawn.

He looked me straight in the eye.

"There's been a fair trial," he said. "The accused has been found innocent. There'll be no posse or lynching party in Deadwood while I'm sheriff."

Not Charlie or me or any of the others who were raring to string Jack McCall up were able to get out that saloon door until Jack McCall had time to make his getaway.

When we was finally able to get past Seth, Charlie and me headed for Digger Dixon's store.

Harry was still there watching over the body. Digger'd laid Bill out real nice in a pine coffin. The lid was off and I could see Bill was still wearing his two Colts in his sash. Digger'd covered over the hole in Bill's chest with a napkin same color as his shirt.

"Wouldn't Wild Bill wanna be buried with his rifle, too?" Harry asked.

"Yep," Charlie answered. "He sure as fuck would. I'll go get it. And I wanna put it there in my pardner's coffin myself."

"I'll be back with something else he'd want in there," I said.

So while Charlie went to get Wild Bill's rifle, I hied me over to the Gem, bought a bottle of Old Potrero Rye Whiskey, and brought it back to Digger Dixon's. Wild Bill Hickok went to meet his maker armed with his trusty weapons and with his favorite booze.

. . . . .

Wild Bill Hickok was buried at Ingleside. Reverend Smith ran the show. I wasn't there. Neither was Colorado Charlie. We were holding our own service at the Little Bonanza getting shitfaced drunk.

There at the Little Bonanza I extracted a promise from Charlie.

"Now that Wild Bill's gone," I told him. "There's only one thing I want."

"What's that, Calam?" he asked.

"When my number's up, I wanna be buried next to my husband. Will you see to that, Charlie?"

"If I'm still alive to see it done, Calam, you got my promise. Your body and Wild Bill's will be side by side forever."

It was after the funeral was over and everyone had left the cemetery that Colorado Charlie and me staggered up to Ingleside. We didn't bring no flowers or nothing to the graveside. What we did was water it with our tears. And neither of us was ashamed of blubbering there over Wild Bill Hickok's fucking grave.

. . . . .

Charlie and me went on a two-week drunk like you wouldn't believe. It probably wasn't a very pretty bender. We was probably pretty sloppy, pretty weepy, and pretty God damned obnoxious. You wanna make something of it?

Our best friend, Colorado Charlie's truest pardner, my own beloved pardner, lover, and husband had been brutally murdered. And the cocksucking fake judge and jury let the snot-nose, shit-mouthed motherfucker who plugged him off free to run around and brag 'bout how he'd killed Wild Bill Hickok. Jesus! Makes me puke just to think 'bout it.

Finally, the two of us sobered up enough so's we could think 'bout evening up the score with that no good son of a bitch Moccasin Varnes, who'd paid twenty bucks to Jack McCall to shoot Wild Bill in the back.

What we did was, we went down to Chinatown to talk to Sam Fat. Colorado Charlie was on terms with Sam so Sam didn't pull none of that phony accent on us. Well, he had an accent, all right. But it was like the people from England have when they speak our language.

"Moccasin Varnes paid Jack McCall to kill our pardner, Wild Bill Hickok," Charlie said.

"Yes," Sam Fat agreed. "I have heard as much from my sources."

Jumping Jesus! Sam Fat really *did* seem to know what was going on behind every closed door in Deadwood.

"Could we arrange with Tom Ng to pay that fuck-ass Varnes back?" Charlie asked.

"I have not heard how much Mister Varnes paid Mister McCall for the service he rendered," Sam Fat admitted.

"Twenty bucks," Charlie told him.

"I am only a humble go-between for the tongs of my community," Tom said. "I do not make deals or break deals. Thus, I have no responsibility for the actions of the Sung tong or the Yee tong. Besides that, you are doubtless aware that there are many acts of violence that occur in Deadwood for which we Chinese are unjustly blamed.

"I would not want you to think that we sons of China favor violence in any way. Our philosophers Confucius and Lao-Tsu teach us that the principle of Peace overrules that of Violence."

"I respect the teachings handed down to your people from the great philosophers," Charlie said. "How much might it cost, though, to right a great injustice?"

"Lao-tsu informs us that the best man is like water," Sam Fat said.

"I assure you, Wild Bill was the best man in these parts," Charlie said.

"Water is good," Sam Fat replied. "It benefits all things and does not compete with them. It dwells in lowly places that all disdain. That is why it is so near the Tao."

"Might twenty dollars be near the Tao?" Charlie asked.

Jesus Christ! What the fuck were them two talking 'bout?

"Confucius teaches us that to go beyond is as wrong as to fall short," Sam Fat said.

"Which means more than twenty dollars would be too much and less than twenty dollars too little?" Charlie asked.

Sam Fat held out his hand. Colorado Charlie plunked twenty bucks into that delicate hand.

"Wind over the lake is the image of inner truth," Sam said.

"Amen," I said.

.....

Now I want you pilgrims to know that I have no idea who did it, or how it happened. But two days after our meeting with Sam Fat, Johnnie Moccasin Varnes was found dead in his bed with a God damned hatchet buried in his skull.

Nobody fucks with Calamity Jane or what's Calamity Jane's.

Which I guess is another way of saying 'Wind over the lake is the image of inner truth.'

That took care of Moccasin Varnes. I guess you all know what happened to Jack McCall, don't you? He was caught by United States Marshall Balcombe on August twenty-ninth. He was tried in Yankton Court House December fourth. And on January third, 1877, he was sentenced to hang.

But that's a whole other story. And it's only part of my revenge on the little cocksucker.

.....

Colorado Charlie spent the time between McCall's escape from Deadwood and his trial at Yankton on a scouting trip to see if McCall really did have a brother.

Turned out he did have one after all. And Charlie and I used that brother as our personal revenge on Jack McCall afore the U.S. Government gave him a suspended sentence. Know what I mean?

It's too long a story to go into right now. I've 'bout talked myself out. And I've developed a thirst that won't quit. So I could use a drink right now. And then I'll be on my way to get me some shuteye.

But there's one thing I wanna leave with you pilgrims afore I go. Nobody, but nobody fucks with Calamity Jane or what's hers. And don't you never fucking forget it.

About the Author

TIM DESMONDES

Tim Desmondes lives in a beach town in Southern California.

His idea of a good time is to sit on his balcony at sundown, his wife at his side and a cold drink in his hand as the golden orb sinks slowly into the Pacific.

His view of Paradise is to glimpse the rare green flash at that cataclysmic moment.

Tim Desmondes is also the author of:

- *Sex and Loathing in Hollywood*
- *Sexual Diversity and Perversity in California*
- *Dracula Sucks Hollywood Dudes*
- *Venus Does Adonis While Apollo Shags a Tree*
- *Arthur Does Camelot*

These books and more are available at Amazon.com, TheNazcaPlainsCorp.com, or your local bookstore.

www.ingramcontent.com/pod-product-compliance
Lightning Source LLC
Chambersburg PA
CBHW071220260626
47162CB00004B/1365
9781934625866